I0545538

JACK
AND THE
VANDALS

A Jack of All Trades novel

DH Smith

Earlham Books

Published 2025 by Earlham Books
Book design & cover art: Lia at NewRadical

Text copyright © 2025 DH Smith

This is a work of fiction. Names, characters,
businesses, places, events and incidents are either
the products of the author's imagination or used
in a fictitious manner. Any resemblance to
actual persons, living or dead, or events
is purely coincidental.

All Rights Reserved

ISBN: 978-1-909804-68-5

Characters

Jack Bell	*builder/private investigator*
Mia Bell	*his daughter, student*
Alison Bell	*Mia's mother, a headteacher*

The Ffrench family:

Robert	*father, deceased, owned a local pharmacy chain*
Judy	*daughter, an event organiser*
Cliff	*son, an artist*
Maggie	*daughter, singer-songwriter, engaged to Mo Bukhari*
Tom	*son, works in advertising*
Lily Brown	*housekeeper, lives nearby*
Mo Bukhari	*civil servant, engaged to Maggie*
Alec Hoskins	*family friend, manager of Ffrenchco*

DI Fayyad Kamani	*Detective Inspector, Forest Gate police station*
DS Nova Taylor	*Detective Sergeant, works with DI Kamani*
Mr Dobbs	*a landlord*

Chapter 1

Jack was seated, on the one chair in the room, at a paint-stained table in paint-stained overalls, head in hands. A hammer, drill, saw, with an open box of screws were on the wooden table, along with a large unopened bottle of whisky. Not a good look, if someone came in.

The turmoil of last night overwhelmed him. Overrated him, as if he were the star of a disaster movie, instead of a bit player, his tiny scene on the cutting room floor.

He had work. So what? Too much work for too little cash. So what was unusual? He was upstairs at a stationer's. His job was to repair and make a flat from the neglected space. One room to be a kitchen-cum-sitting room, another a bathroom with a shower somehow to be fitted into its limited space, and the third a bedroom. Repair, paint the walls white, the doors brown.

Last night's movie was playing on, as if on repeat. He had hardly slept, going over the scene in the restaurant, the key scene, word by word, cutting, deleting, but ending up with the same exit line.

Time heals, he would be told. He'd said it himself. Cliches come easy to the contented. He was hungry, but he couldn't move. Not even to open the bottle, his last pennies invested in the poisonous liquid. Getting here was as much as he could manage. Here he would stay, rot, feed the life that lives off life. Bacteria, fungi, flies, grubs; he was their sustenance. The day too long, the light too much, too late to crawl back into the coffin.

Max, his mentor, said eschew self pity. But take that away and what was left of him?

Yesterday, he was someone, hopeful, on the verge of the future he'd constructed. He had spent nearly all his money on the ring. He must get comatose, wipe away the memory of yesterday, today and tomorrow. The only sensible state, senselessness. And throw the ring in the river. Let it sink forever in the mud.

It was just out of reach, the lifesaver. Jack rose, turned away from the sun glaring on the bottle, a useless warning for a shipwrecked sailor, already on the rocks. Outside the traffic rumbled, going where, going for what discernable reason?

What was the point? The reason behind anything.

He mustn't get drunk. He must get drunk. A rejected lover tearing the petals of a buttercup. Trying not to look at the bottle.

But what else was there to do? Fix the floorboards. So what? He didn't have a glass. So what? He could borrow one from downstairs. But why be posh?

Jack picked up the bottle to unscrew the lid. He'd down it in one long draught. Let the world go hang. The top was too tight; he grimaced and twisted it. Then gave up. He considered smashing the head off, but that would be difficult to drink from and spill everywhere. Right, think straight, he would give the lid a sharp tap with his hammer. His new found meaning. Jack went to his toolbox and took out a claw hammer, stroking the steel head, just as there was a rap on the door, and a call:

'Hello. Anyone in there?'

Called back to the well-mannered world, he put the bottle under the table, looked about the room. Expecting nobody. Not his client, Mr Dobbs, besides which the voice had been female.

'Come in,' he said, putting down the hammer, so he wouldn't look quite so threatening.

A woman tentatively entered. Medium height, slim, light brown hair to her shoulders, blue jeans and a red T-shirt with *Get Over It* imprinted in gothic black. A light brown leather, expensive looking handbag on a long strap over her shoulder.

She looked around the room, screwing up her nose at the dust.

'Are you Jack Bell,' she said doubtfully.

He might have challenged this, knowing who he was yesterday, but today he hadn't been confirmed.

'Who wants him?' he said.

She looked about the room again, seeing two doors. 'Would you get him for me, please.'

How might he conjure a self into being? He flipped the on switch.

'I'm Jack Bell.' There, he'd admitted himself. Joined the human race, sort of.

She looked him up and down, and shook her head.

'You are not exactly selling yourself.'

He smiled wryly. 'My daughter says, if I knew how to market, I might yet make a bad living.'

She laughed. 'You are doing all the wrong things, Mr Bell. You are supposed to shake my hand and exude confidence. Instead of signalling cut-price, cheap jack.'

He might've said, 'Got me in two.' But he swallowed that rejoinder and said, 'How did you know I was here?'

'Your curious website. Forest Gate Investigations.'

He'd almost forgotten that still existed, gathering cobwebs in the far corner of the internet.

'I phoned. A young woman answered,' she went on, 'and told me you were here. I tried to call you. You'll hear my message on your voicemail. Getting no reply, and not being far, I came up.'

He attempted hospitality mode.

'Would you like a seat?' Offering the one chair, for what reason, he could hardly fathom. Politeness or something.

'No.' She put out her hand. 'Judy Ffrench. Two fs.'

'Why two?'

She laughed. 'To confuse people.'

Good teeth, quite attractive which meant he was becoming more human by the minute. It wouldn't last, as soon as she was gone he'd go too.

3

'This is not the most comfortable place to talk, I'm afraid...' he said.

He had half an idea of going up the road to Costa Coffee, but he had no money after buying the booze. He could hardly ask her to lend him a tenner.

'I can hardly believe it,' she exclaimed, blowing out her cheeks. 'You are not sure who you are and I find you in this dump.'

'This is not my office,' he said, knowing he had to climb out of the hole she was looking into. 'I'm a builder as well as a private investigator.'

She sucked her bottom lip. 'Could be useful,' she mused. Then added, 'Perhaps. Let's go to Costa.'

'I've come out without cash,' he said.

'Marketing for Dummies,' she said, throwing up her hands. 'Boy oh boy!'

He was getting angry. Which was at least a step up from self pity.

'I don't know what you want,' he said, 'but I wasn't expecting you, and so...'

'Your phone was off.'

'I was busy.' He didn't say staring at a whisky bottle.

'Let's go to Costa,' she said. 'I'll pay.' Adding, 'Bring your tool box.'

'Why?'

'Just a thought I have. Bear with me. I might yet be your client.'

Jack considered for a few seconds whether to leave the items on the table, the hammer, drill, saw and screws. But decided to pack them, as you never know, becoming a builder by the minute, with a faint odour of the private eye. As they were leaving, he picked up the whisky bottle, saying to Judy, 'Won it in a raffle.'

Once in the shop downstairs, he said the same to Mr Patel behind the counter, adding, 'I don't drink. Have it on me.'

Booze handed over, he left the shop with the woman with two fs.

Chapter 2

He and Judy sat by the window overlooking the high street, choosing a table for two, away from the other customers. She went to get the hot drinks. The coffee shop was new, just open a year or so. What had it been before? New build, this whole block, but what had it been? So easy to forget. Of course, the butcher, whatshisname. He clicked his fingers. Barry's! All gone in the demolition, along with a luggage shop, a betting shop, a Greggs bakery.

All makes work. Was that the why of it? The reason behind it all.

It was mid morning, the customers were mostly women, three pushchairs, an infant running about. The sun was in his eyes, he moved his chair. But it would catch him in a few minutes.

Seeing a woman eating a roll, he was aware how hungry he was. He'd had no breakfast, nor dinner last night when he'd left the restaurant when Nova rejected his proposal. The recollection was a punch of misery. He had been stupidly sure she would accept. She had been so nice the last few days, agreeable, happy. But then the killer blow, she was seeing someone, she told him...

Judy came over with a tray which she placed on the table. Two coffees in china cups, sachets of sugar in the saucer, two currant-laden, sugary pastries on separate plates. They took their cups and plates, she put the tray on a nearby table, while he emptied the sachets into his coffee and attacked the pastry. All the wrong grub for his diabetes. Sugar, sugar, and more sugar. There was too much of it around. In everything. And he was addicted.

'This place is so bland,' she said. 'Look at this furniture, like school lunch tables. And the music they play, pop rubbish. I suppose the whole chain gets the same stuff. But at least we can talk without being overheard.' She sighed. 'Just a sight better than that depressing flat you are working on.'

He didn't find this place bad. It was a coffee bar. Sure, a bit samey, but lots of room, no one bothering them. But you don't argue with a client. Not a 'customer', that's what his daughter told him. Client. Shops have customers, said Mia. Builders and private eyes have clients.

'You are hungry,' she exclaimed watching him gorge. She hadn't touched her pastry while he'd almost finished his.

'Sorry.' He wiped his mouth with a tissue. 'I normally have a fry up mid morning,' he said. 'After a couple of hours work.' Joke, work being a euphemism for being in the workplace. 'Then I hit the calories.'

Having finished his pastry, a little satisfied but still hungry. She could see him eyeing her pastry.

'Have it,' she said, pushing it across.

'You sure?'

'I only bought it to keep you company.' She grimaced. 'Too much sugar for me. Tooth rot.'

Which reminded him he must go to the dentist. He'd had a toothache, that came and went, dulled with aspirin. Cheaper than the dentist, but he couldn't delay it much longer.

'Eat,' she said, 'while I fill you in. First though, tell me, what are your rates?'

He swallowed, cleared his mouth, took a swig of coffee while he tried to recall the charges that he and Mia had conjured up.

'Two fifty a day,' he said.

'And if I employed you as a builder too?'

That was intriguing, and maybe accounted for being asked to bring the toolbox. Jack contemplated what sum he could set. He didn't want to price himself out, nor be too cheap.

'Depends,' he said, 'on the building work you want, as well as the investigation.' Giving himself more thinking time.

'Two thousand pounds,' she said. 'Starting tomorrow. But I want a result by Saturday at the latest.'

Startled, he tried not to react, as if it was an everyday amount. But the timetable was tight. By Saturday. Too tight? How on earth could he know? But it was a hefty amount. It would more than do. Though Mr Dobbs would kick up a fuss when he left the job above the shop. Just for the rest of the week, though. He'd do as much as he could today, then have to pop in and out. Do a bit whenever he could. Where does she live? She'd walked here, so couldn't be far off. She'd get most of his time, of course, for whatever she wanted. Two thou. She had outpriced Dobbs for sure, but he'd have to work night and day.

Just don't get too excited.

'That's agreeable,' he said, hoping he sounded cool, trying not to grab the cash with both hands. But suppose he didn't get a result. How could that be guaranteed?

'Half up front?' he said, thinking that at least he'd have that, result or not.

She nodded, and he went on, 'You'd best tell me what exactly you want from me.'

'You are almost sounding professional, Jack.'

He smiled. Two cakes munched, half the coffee drunk, whisky bottle given away, he was almost in builder-detective mode. Never quite believing in it.

'Give me the low down.' he said.

Even as he said it, he knew he was playing Hollywood cop. Noir, as Nova told him when they saw that Bogart movie. When would she leave him alone?

Judy took a swig of coffee, looked about her to make sure no one was too close. Though with the music, you'd need to be pretty close. She leaned forward, and spoke softly, so he had to strain to hear.

'My brother, Cliff, has been jailed for murder. He's in Pentonville, on remand, awaiting trial.'

Jack couldn't quell a shudder, which he hoped she took as sympathy. The memory of jail: the barnyard stench, the violence, the screws giving orders, the noise day and night, the petty regulations. But the smell overall, the human zoo.

'You believe he's innocent,' he managed to say, hiding his memories of Pentonville.

'Yes.' And sighed. 'The stupid idiot confessed.'

His ears pricked up, cogs whirring; the vision of a man sitting on the lower bunk bed, trying not to kill his fellow inmate. Aware he was breathing rapidly, he took a drink of coffee and counted three before daring to answer.

'Your brother either has a death wish,' he said, working at keeping calm. 'Or he's protecting someone.'

Or he's guilty, he thought.

'You are not just a two-bit builder,' she said with a smile.

He almost came back with a two thousand pound one, but saw that as too cheeky as he hadn't yet got this signed and sealed.

'Those are the options,' he said instead. 'For Cliff Ffrench?' She nodded at the surname. No great guess, Cliff was after all her brother. 'Who's the victim?'

'Our father,' she said. 'Richard Ffrench. Murdered two months ago, at the house where I live on Osborne Road.'

The road was just opposite. It hosted Forest Gate Festival every summer. He and Nova had gone there, last year, a street festival, stalls all along the road. Wasn't it coming up soon? He'd seen a poster somewhere. Nova said they should go. Jack clenched his fists beneath the table. Was every memory going to be contaminated?

'You need to come to the house,' she said. 'It isn't far up the road.' She pointed across the street. 'It'll make the explanation clearer.'

She rose. He drank the last of his coffee, stood and picked up his toolbox.

Chapter 3

They crossed Woodgrange high street at the lights, and headed down Osborne, along the hoarding around the empty Methodist church.

'Do you think they'll ever get building?' she said, indicating the graffiti-plastered hoarding.

He shrugged. 'It's a racket. The developers have no intention of building. Must be six years empty now. They keep selling on, as property prices rise, to another developer who does the same thing.' He smiled. 'Not my league.'

'Bunch of shysters.'

She was walking a little faster than him. He struggled to keep up, encumbered with the toolbox.

'Why the tight timetable?' he said.

She stopped. 'I know the way you guys work. String it out for more cash. I reckon if you don't get a quick result, you won't get any result.'

He was unsure of the logic of that. But why argue? He'd at least get a thousand, and might get a result. He'd try like hell. And get the two thou.

'What's the story with the bottle of whisky?'

Some quick thinking needed.

'Won it in a raffle.' Too quick. Like this job.

'So why take it into work?'

He half smiled to hide his discomfort. Quick lies lead to trouble.

'I was going to sell it.'

She shook her head. 'No, you weren't. Level with me.'

Jack thought for a few seconds. They were standing outside the gate of the nursery school, in the shade of a tree growing in the grounds. They could hear the kids yelling but not see them as the fence was covered in a privet hedge.

He was going to lose the job if he wasn't careful.

'When you were packing your tools, I found this,' she said. She unravelled a receipt from the Co-op. He didn't need to look at the detail. £19.99 whisky.

He shrugged. She had him. Did he have a big enough lie to envelop everything? The master of all lies.

No.

'My girlfriend dumped me last night,' he said, deciding to come clean. He might lose the job, but if he carried on lying, he definitely would. 'I proposed to her, in the Himalaya, up Stratford.'

'I know it,' she said. 'Let's carry on walking.'

'A bit slower,' he said. 'The toolbox is heavy.'

'Sorry. I'll keep to your pace.'

They walked side by side.

'I'd bought a ring,' he went on. 'We've been going out a couple of years, and I thought, let's go for it. Except when I brought out the ring, she told me she'd met someone. A woman as it happens. Not that it makes any difference. She's a cop. Not that that makes any difference either.'

'Fed up with men.'

'Well, me anyway. I didn't stay to eat. She called after me to explain, but I really didn't want to hear the just good friends pitch.'

'I know the feeling. So you bought the bottle intending to get plastered.'

'That's the size of it. Took the last of my cash, just about.'

'That's why I had to get the coffee,' she said. Jack didn't reply. 'When was the last time you got drunk?'

'More than a year ago. I don't drink as a rule.'

'Except when you get dumped.'

He stopped. 'If you want to pull me off the job, I get it. But don't give me the third degree.'

She looked at him, bit her bottom lip. 'I can't deal with a drunk, Jack. I've got enough problems.'

'So is that it?'

'Let's go to the house, while I think about it.'

They continued down the road in silence, Judy keeping his pace. They were on the south side of the road, the sun high in the sky. He was overdressed, feeling sweaty round the collar, and tired. He yawned. A vision of Nova struck him, in the restaurant, telling him how touched she was by his proposal, and what a beautiful ring, but... Like a guillotine. The but.

Time heals. Except when it doesn't.

Keep walking. Remember you are alive, said Max. Screw self pity.

The houses along the road were semi-detached, double fronted, Victorian, two storeys. This was the conservation area. Expensive housing. Any repairs had to be in keeping with the original style. Jack had done a couple of jobs in the area, so knew the restrictions.

He said, for something to say, to break the awkwardness: 'Forest Gate Festival is on this road. Must be soon.'

'Saturday,' she said grimly. 'And I'm organising a wedding on the day. Not mine, my sister's. With Dad dead, I said to her, cancel it. Out of respect. It's too close. She said, no, I'm two months pregnant. I'm not waiting.'

She laughed wryly. 'I'm an event organiser. The wedding is a tiddly thing in my book. 80 guests, I'm used to thousands. But everything was a muddle with Dad's murder. The police were everywhere in the house, and questioning us night and day. Then arresting Cliff. He's my twin, I am older by an hour. Big sister. Like hell I am. They wouldn't release Dad's body for weeks. We only had the funeral three weeks ago. Go for it, says my sister, I need to be married. We had a row half the night. Dad murdered, Cliff in jail, how can we have a wedding! She said if I wouldn't do it, she'd hire a wedding organiser. So I gave in. I thought what the heck.

'You've got to laugh. Dad's been murdered, Cliff awaiting trial, and so we have a wedding on the day of the festival. How apt is that?'

'A little unfortunate timing,' he said.

'So the day after the funeral, can you believe, I am hassling to get a marquee, last minute stuff, summer is peak for marquees, you pay through the nose. But I know people, and they know to keep me sweet. Give me this, I'll give you that for the Suffolk festival, so the marquee is coming Thursday. And then parking...' She threw up her hands. 'This street has to be cleared for the festival!'

'There's stalls both sides of the road,' he said.

Recalling the myriad stalls, arts, crafts, clothing, scouts, all the community groups, masses for kids, plenty of food, two sound stages, last year when he came with Nova and Mia. Mia had persuaded him to put his head through the clown's face and have wet sponges thrown at him. He'd even considered having a stall himself, as Forest Gate Investigations, but Mia said it'd be a waste of time.

'We got a leaflet through the door,' said Judy. 'All cars have to be off the street by midnight Friday.' She threw up her hands. 'And I have 80 guests, half of them driving here. So I've paid up for 40 parking tickets. What a palaver! Not that that allows them to park on the road, oh no, but on side streets, wherever they can find.' She shrugged. 'There's always something you haven't thought about.'

'The guests might enjoy the festival.'

She grinned. 'So they might. If the caterers don't show up. Perhaps I could book the main stage for the ceremony. The Dog Jammers playing *Here Comes the Bride*.'

He had friends in the Dog Jammers. Big group, who didn't?

She stopped and opened the garden gate. The house was double frontage, yellow brickwork, big urns of white and red flowers on either side of the door.

He followed her to the door. She could talk for England, but that suited him in his mood. But he did need to wake himself up. Contribute something for all that cash. If she didn't strike him out for the whisky bottle.

Chapter 4

They went into the kitchen. Jack put down the toolbox by the long kitchen island and looked about him. Nothing awry in this well-appointed kitchen: saucepans suspended on hooks from a long rail above the island, marble worktops round the walls, a fridge and freezer, a dishwasher, a six ring oven, and hordes of dark brown wooden cupboards, what did they keep in them all? Matching shelving, a microwave oven, an air fryer. He was trying to ascertain what work he could do here, but everything was in good repair. He crossed to the double sink by the back window, where he could make out the planking of the patio, a lawn beyond, flower beds at the edges and at the rear a shed. Turning back to the kitchen; it was still near perfect.

'This is so tidy, it's almost frightening,' said Jack, almost scared to touch anything. Being the one untidy item in his paint-stained overalls and work boots.

'Lily cleans for us. Two hours every morning. Not our bedrooms, they are a tip, but the communal rooms.'

'Who lives here?' he said, seating himself on one of the four stools along the island.

'Well, me, I moved in a month ago.' She sat down. 'I've let out my flat in the Bow Quarter.'

'Wasn't that the old Match Factory by Bow Bridge?'

'So it says on the plaque at the gate. Where was I? Maggie, my sister, the one getting married, has the front bedroom, and Mo, her fiance, seems to be a fixture. And there's Tom, my other brother, the one not in jail, though more by luck than judgement.'

'Three of you,' he said, attempting to keep track. 'Sister and brother along with you,' he said. 'Plus Mo the groom, who is here most of the time. The murder, though, was two months ago. Who was here then?'

'It was after a family dinner. Dad went off to have a nap in his bedroom, he tires easily, and said he'd be down later, but he never came down. It was his 70th birthday. We wanted to do something grander but he wouldn't have it. Too many birthdays already, he said. So, who was here then?' She enumerated on her fingers, 'Me, Maggie, Cliff, Tom, Dad, Mo – Maggie's add-on. And Uncle Alec, he's Dad's friend and manager of his business. Junior partner, you might say. They've known each other for 50 years. And Lily did the cooking.'

'What was your father's business?'

'He owned 12 chemist shops in East London, Uncle Alec has 10%. You might have seen Ffrenchco branches, though there isn't one in Forest Gate. The nearest is Ilford, no, Stratford.' She shrugged, 'Now we have his share, us Ffrenchies, and the house too. We've done alright. All except Cliff, that is.'

'What about your mother?'

'She died 15 years ago of breast cancer.' She stood up. 'Let me show you the house before the others get back.'

'Where are they?'

'Maggie, Mo and Tom are off doing wedding business. Sorting out flowers, picking up printing, getting the dress. You know, bits and pieces. I sit around chasing things up and delegate. Let me show you the room where it happened.'

They left the kitchen, into the wide hallway and up the stairs. He followed her along the landing. Jack put a hand on her shoulder and stopped her.

'Whose are these rooms?'

'That's my room at the back of the house. Bathroom next to it. This one here is Tom's room. Do you want to see inside?'

'Yes, I need to get the lie of the house.'

14

'It's a tip,' she said, 'a jumble of his clothes.' She turned the handle twice and back. 'He's locked it.' She turned to him, saying with some reluctance, 'Do you want to see mine.'

Did he? But he couldn't just be nice, as it might be revealing. 'Yes.'

They went back along the landing to her room. She opened the door, the sun was streaming in, the yellow blinds up, onto a large unmade bed. He came into the room and looked out of the window. The patio roof was below.

'I should open the window,' she said sniffing, 'but I don't like insects coming in.'

He almost said, there's 50% less insects due to habitat loss and climate change, as Mia had informed him, but quelled it and looked about the room.

It was large; other than the bed, there was a wardrobe, a chest of drawers, and a dressing table with central and side mirrors. A large colourful abstract was on the wall. There was a small TV and amplifier, in an alcove, a bookshelf full of books and by it a low ladder, presumably to reach the top shelves. In an opposite alcove were two filing cabinets, one labelled A to K, the other L to Z. On top of one, two barbells, and on the other a tower of extra weights. For decoration, he wondered, or does she push iron?

Two pairs of Nike trainers almost under the bed.

'Do you run?' he said.

'Every day,' she said. 'I did the London Marathon. Broke three hours.'

'That's good,' he said. Not knowing whether it was or not, but she was obviously pleased with the time.

Jack glanced at the books. Some children's books at the bottom, and quite a few crime novels. The others meant nothing to him. Just books, those scary things that threatened him in the library.

'I feel so revealed,' she said. 'My mess, my things. Is that enough for you?'

'Sorry,' he said.

'Enough. Let me show you where it happened.' She ushered him out of her room, blew out her cheeks. 'I feel like I have been standing there naked while you looked me up and down.'

'Rooms say a lot about us,' he said.

'Don't tell me what mine says,' she said, flapping her hands. 'I must look at yours some time.'

Jack doubted that was an offer. Just a way of shoving off her discomfort.

She led him to the master bedroom at the front of the house. Judy twisted the handle.

'And this one is locked too.' She shrugged. 'Not that there would be much to see. Dad was strangled in there by a length of wire. He was found dead, lying on the bed, by Lily in the morning. We got rid of the bed. Well, no one wanted to sleep in it. Had a thorough clean up of the room once the cops had gone through everything. All the furniture and rugs got rid of. It was a shell. We redecorated. Dad's clothes have gone to charity shops, his papers and stuff are in the loft.' She pointed above her head, where there was a trapdoor in the ceiling.

'I might want to take a look at those.'

She grimaced. 'Anything that goes up there, stays up there. It's dusty and spidery, and packed tight. Do you really think there might be something useful in his papers?'

Jack shrugged, recalling what Nova told him; ninety per cent of an investigation was simply clearing things away, so you can get to the ten percent that mattered.

'Who knows?' he said.

'I'd hate to get that lot down,' she said looking up at the trap door. 'Not now though. Let's have a coffee and a chat about how you might operate.'

They went down the stairs to the kitchen.

Jack sat at the island while she prepared the coffee. He wondered whether she would take him on or not. That whisky bottle between them. Had he spent 20 quid to lose 2000? Pretty bad odds, that. He needed a reference. Not

Nova, though she owed him one. He'd never ever ask her for anything, not till the seas ran dry. There was Fayyad, her boss and his mate, dating back to his schooldays. A detective inspector at Forest Gate cop shop, and so well dressed, as if he was the best man at a wedding. A good friend, and Jack had helped him a number of times.

'If I gave you the job,' she said, 'working here and observing us over the next few days. Do you think you could find out who really killed Dad? No, forget that. How can you possibly know in advance. So tell me, what building work would you do in your undercover role?'

Jack noted the 'if' and the 'would'. Maybe words, like he was being interviewed. That damned bottle. Booze always gets you in trouble, said Max. You spend your life apologising. And wasn't that the truth. It wasn't as if he had had even a drop of it. Just being seen with it was enough.

She was looking at him, waiting. He recalled the question.

'I haven't seen anything that needs work in this house. Might be some outside,' he said indicating the patio and garden. 'Though this would be the best room by far. Everyone comes into the kitchen. Makes coffee and perhaps a sandwich, would sit down a while, be easy to chat to. To ask me what I am doing, or how much longer I am going to be.' He thought of his van with *Jack of All Trades* on the side, that was always good for wisecracks that he'd heard a hundred times. 'Except this room is perfect. I don't see a scratch anywhere. It's the sort of kitchen that goes in a magazine.'

Judy grimaced. He wasn't sure what about. Was it the lack of work or his taunt about the kitchen? In spite of her grimace, which he'd noted a few times, she was attractive. Strong, those weights, the running, a full body. Judy ate well, and it settled in the right places.

She poured the hot water into the cafetière, as if she had a grudge against it.

'Can you give me a reference,' she said, as if she had been reading his thoughts.

'Detective Inspector Fayyad Kamani at Forest Gate police station.' Glad that he'd anticipated it.

'Can I phone him?'

'Sure.'

Both took out their phones and he gave her the number.

'OK, you go outside, Jack, for five minutes while I call him and the coffee settles. I don't want you listening in. See the house from out there. The patio, the brickwork, the windows, the shed, must be something needs doing. Think how you might go about it. Go!'

Given his marching orders, Jack left via the kitchen garden-door, and closed it behind him. A glance back told him she was phoning. Let's hope Fayyad is in, he thought. He watched her, on the stool at the island, the phone to her ear. She waved him away, just as she began speaking.

He crossed his fingers and walked around the patio. The decking was in good condition. It could always do with a varnish. Except he'd have to do it overnight, as she had a marquee coming in a few days, with lots of crossings of the patio, back and forth, as the garden had no side entrance. There was a roof over the patio, making it more of a verandah. The roof had obviously been repaired recently, as if there was a conspiracy to deny him work.

There was a wooden table on the patio that could seat six, with folded chairs stacked on the ground. A two seat sofa at one end, a bit sunken, could do with upholstering, but not a job for him.

Jack glanced at the kitchen. He could see Judy still talking on the phone, quite animated, asking searching questions maybe. About his drinking perhaps. He so rarely got drunk these days, but most surely he would have done this morning, if Judy hadn't turned up. Or suppose he'd been working here, what then?

Out here, alone, a wave of misery hit him. Rejection was like a kick in the guts, and then recurring echoes. Even now, the morning after, he was shaky. Work, stick to the job. Time heals and all that flimflam. He stepped out onto the lawn and looked back at the house.

Judy's room, extended two thirds of the way across the house, and then the bathroom. The patio roof was in good repair, and, stepping further back, so was the house roof, ditto the guttering and downpipe. He turned to the side and looked at the wooden fencing, newish on both sides. He crossed to have a closer look. Just a few years old. Besides which, working out here would be useless. He had to be chatting to people, not working out here on his own. In fact, the work hardly mattered when it came down to it. It was the chatting, the interactions.

His real job was to get Cliff off. That's if Fayyad was saying all the right things and he got the work.

Flowers in the beds along both fences. Colourful, but he had no idea what they were. Not his thing, flowers.

Jack strolled to the shed at the back corner of the garden. Quite large. A lock on the door, but it wasn't locked. He opened up. Surprisingly tidy inside. They must have a gardener. Tools hung up neatly, a mower. A bench for potting. Some carpentry tools on shelves: a drill, saws, jars of nails and screws, and oddments. Sacking with fertilizer, or so it said on the bag. Small boxes on a shelf of weedkillers and pesticides, but her father had been strangled, not poisoned.

Then he saw the coil of wire under the potting table. He picked up the coil and felt the wire for flexibility. Bendy enough. Get a length round someone's neck and pull hard. He shuddered.

Could a length of this have been used? But this wire was as common as chips. And most likely the murderer had taken his piece away with him. But something to check on.

Jack left the shed, closing the door. They do need to lock it. Tools are stolen, some pricey stuff in there. He shrugged. Too much money in this family. He crossed the lawn, heading back to the house for his coffee and Judy's verdict after talking to Fayyad.

As he drew close, he could see Judy smashing at the kitchen cupboards with his hammer. What on earth was she doing?

Chapter 5

The kitchen door was locked. She continued hammering away, as he shook the door and shouted, smashing at the cupboards and shelves, the floor was a paving of china shards. Jack rapped on the window, he called, but she continued her demolition. He watched horrified as she smashed and hammered, at perfectly good, very expensive cupboards. Top range, never had he had to fit that quality.

He couldn't watch and sat on the small sofa, but could hear the bashing, rhythmic, as if she was dancing about the room, hammer in hand, muffled through the double glazing. Had she gone mad? Her secret. His booze, her destruction, both out in the open. Should he phone someone? An ambulance? Paramedics with a straitjacket?

It came to him as the hammering stopped. The silence was thunderous. She was making work for him. Surely not? He daren't look. Perhaps she was taking a breather, gearing up for a second round. Or might she smash him, having done all the cupboards and shelves.

And then Judy came out, her hair awry, ceramic chips in her hair. She was carrying a tray with mugs of coffee and a biscuit tin. How had she been able to protect it amidst her carnage?

'Let's sit at the table,' she said.

Judy's face was sweaty but she seemed calm, not like the mad axe woman he'd seen through the kitchen window.

He got two chairs from the stack and unfolded them at the table where she placed the tray, putting out the coffees, the small plates, and opening the biscuit tin as if it had been an uneventful morning and this was their elevenses.

Both sat down. She smiled at him, a little shyly. She was strong, she'd just had a workout.

'You run,' he recalled.

'Good listener.' She put a finger up. 'Oh yes, you're a detective.'

'Quick recovery from the kitchen action.'

'I run every morning at six. Over Wanstead Flats, come rain or come shine. I do cross country and road running with Wanstead AC.'

He thought of inviting her out on the Flats with his telescope one night. Except the kitchen couldn't be ignored.

'Is smashing the kitchen an Olympic event?' he said.

She smiled. 'You said the kitchen was the best place.'

It was as he thought.

'You have been making work?' She nodded. 'A perfectly good kitchen. Heaven help us.' He threw up his hands at the needless destruction.

'The insurance will pay,' she said.

'For you smashing up your kitchen? I don't think so.'

'I have thought it out, Jack. We came back to the house, you and me, went into the kitchen and found it all smashed up...'

'Why would a builder come back with you?'

She looked at him quizzically, then realised. 'You're right, why would I need a builder beforehand. Erase that. I came back on my own, I had been for a run, over the Flats. Got back and I found the kitchen smashed up. So I phoned a builder.'

He nodded. 'That's me in the frame. Then your brother and sister get back. They'd expect you to phone the police, and especially if you are thinking of doing an insurance scam.'

He took a sip of coffee and a shortbread biscuit. He did not want to go into the kitchen and see the extent of the wreckage.

'Forget I said anything about the insurance,' she said.

'You should forget it too.'

'That's my business,' she snapped.

They were quiet for a few seconds.

He said, 'Whatever you do, you have to phone the police. Or your brother and sister will, and they will wonder why you didn't.'

She nodded, and picked up her phone.

'It's not serious enough for 999,' she said. 'The non-urgent number, it has to be, for a minor crime,' she said. 'I've got it somewhere.'

She flipped through her phone. 'Here it is.' She dialled. He watched her. 'I'd like to report a break in,' she said into her phone. She gave the address. 'I came back from a run and found the kitchen all smashed up.'

Jack left her and went to the kitchen door, standing holding the jambs as if for support. With no house pixies to reassemble the damage, it was the mess he had seen her creating, shattered cupboards and shelves, broken china scattered over the floor, wall plaster shattered in places. She had been thorough. Every cupboard and shelf would have to be replaced. He was overwhelmed, a perfect, magazine-ready kitchen desecrated. Where could he get replacement cupboards, how soon? Could be a two-person job, lifting them to secure them. But he knew a weight lifter.

First job, though, clear up. Brooms.

As Jack crossed the garden to the shed, he recalled he still hadn't got the work. She had been considering and then checked on his reference. What had Fayyad said to her? Though she had been more or less suggesting that she was creating work for him. And she'd done that in spades. 2000 quid for the job, but he needed her to confirm he had the job.

He returned from the shed with two outdoor brooms, a shovel and two pairs of leather gloves, which he parked by the kitchen door.

Judy was still at the table, somewhat shell-shocked.

'What's up?'

'I thought, just vandalism, they won't come round,' she said. 'But they're coming over. The officer remembered there was a murder here. He went off to get someone, I could hear this chatter in the background. And the upshot is they'll be here. I asked when, and he said, shortly.'

Jack gave a wry laugh.

'What have I got myself into!' she exclaimed. 'I must stick to my story. I can't think what else to do. You won't drop me in it, will you?'

'Of course not. What happened with the reference?'

'Almost forgot that. Ancient history. DI Fayyad Kamani was in a meeting, but I spoke to a woman who knew you. Nova?'

Jack nodded. It would have to be.

'Nova gave you a brilliant reference. She said you were thoroughly trustworthy and a good investigator. I asked her if you had a problem with drink, and she said, hardly ever.'

'Is hardly ever good enough for you?'

'It'll have to be,' she said. 'You could blackmail me for lying to the cops.' She saw the brooms and shovel. 'We mustn't tidy up. They are sending a forensic team.'

'The full works,' he exclaimed, taken aback. 'Let's think this out. What tools of mine did you use for your demolition?'

'Just the claw hammer. From your toolbox.'

'Give it a scrub, there could be flecks on it. We need to bring my toolbox out of the kitchen, and put it in the shed.'

Chapter 6

They were on the patio. The cops had told her they should stay out of the kitchen.

'Phone me,' he said.

'Why?'

'Now, at once,' he exclaimed. 'They could check your phone, to see if you phoned me to come over when you found the kitchen vandalised. It would make it less likely we were in this together. Phone me. Now.'

He was getting into this too deep. Backing up her lies with his own. Hell's bells. He couldn't afford to get arrested. Could well be a prison sentence if he got caught.

She phoned him, standing six feet away.

'Jack of All Trades,' he said, answering. 'What can I do for you?'

'I need a builder urgently.' He could hear her without the phone. 'My kitchen's been vandalised.'

'I am rather busy.'

She snarled at him and gave him two fingers.

'Two thousand pounds,' she said. 'If you come right away. Or I'll call some other cowboy.'

'Half up front.'

'Whatever you say. Get here!'

She ended the call. Jack did so too.

'Now we just hope the cops are not too quick,' he said. 'Or those calls won't stand up. It would take me ten minutes to get here. Say fifteen, what with packing my tools.'

'They may not ask for my phone first thing,' she said. 'Why should they? And by that time I'd have told them how everyone was out, who lives here, what I came back to and how I then phoned the police and a builder because we have a wedding on Saturday, and go on about how I don't feel safe any longer, that someone must have our front door key and so on. So, unless they have noted the exact time they arrived they wouldn't notice any discrepancy... And would they have?'

'I hope not. It's not murder. Just vandalism.'

'But they said it could be connected to my father's murder.'

'It is in a way.'

'How?'

'It's to make work for me, so I can work away when everyone comes into the kitchen to make coffee, have breakfast, lunch and tea, chat to them about the weather, how West Ham are useless and, by the way, tell me about your dad's murder. And solve the crime. Hey Presto! Like magic.'

She slapped her hands to her face. 'With poor Cliff rotting in jail, while I smash cupboards. You must get him out.'

'I'll do the repairs and I'll investigate.' He didn't feel at all confident that he could solve a crime that the cops thought was already solved. And maybe it was. He'd have to go and see Cliff.

'Two thousand pounds for a week's work, you said,' he added. 'Half up front.'

She nodded, then said, 'Three thousand, if you prove Cliff innocent.'

'I'll do what I can. And while we are waiting for the cops, I'd best be a builder. Where did you get the kitchen cupboards from? We need to make an order.'

'One minute.' She ran into the kitchen.

Contaminating the crime scene. Except her prints and DNA would be all over the kitchen anyway. He had wiped the stool where he'd sat earlier by the kitchen island and the island top, which would have his prints. Though he could easily explain them. He was a builder and had looked at the work to be done, and he was sorry if there was a print here and there.

Judy returned with a booklet of the kitchen cupboards, with the receipt too. He gasped when he saw the amount they had cost. Well, she was paying for this lot. He'd have nothing to do with any insurance fiddle. The receipt conveniently itemised the cupboards, shelving and fittings.

'You'd better re-order that lot,' he said. 'Get it as soon as possible. Sooner, pay extra. With luck, they'll have it all in stock. Get all the fittings too. May not need all of them, but best play safe.'

So easy spending someone else's money, he thought. And realising how well off the family was. Twelve chemist's shops, this house, her father's investments, he was bound to have had some. Money goes to money. Plus she was letting out her flat in Bow and living here rent free.

Though he was getting a little of it. Now that Nova had given him a reference. The least she could do for him. Could he resell the ring? It had cost him £400. Maybe he could just return it to the shop, say it was unsuitable or whatever. Worth a try. No good to him. He had the receipt.

Or save it for next time.

Judy was still on the phone about the cupboards, and gave him the thumbs up. He'd go back to Dobbs' place once the cops had done with him, and do some work there. Have to do something to try to keep Dobbs quiet. Bound to be a row when he realised Jack was on another job. Always was, doing two jobs. Someone not happy.

Jack looked at his watch. Fifteen minutes since she'd phoned the cops. Just about OK for him to have just arrived. What was his toolbox doing in the shed? That wasn't thought out. It was just nerves, wanting to get it far away. But he'd have it with him, if he'd just come.

So easy to make mistakes when you are concocting a story.

He went to the shed and brought his toolbox back, leaving it on the patio. Judy had finished her phone call.

'I'd have my tools with me,' he said. 'If I'd just arrived.'

'They've got everything in stock,' she said. 'They told me three days to get it here. I told them I needed it tomorrow, I had a wedding at the weekend. They said that would need a special delivery, £500. I agreed, paid up and it's all coming in the morning.'

'Let's hope the cops are done with the kitchen by tomorrow, and I can get on with renewing the cupboards.'

She looked at the time on her phone. 'Twenty-two minutes since I phoned you. So we are fine on that.'

'I should go,' he said. 'I mean, I'm just your builder as far as the world is concerned. We've agreed the job. You've ordered the materials. Nothing I can do now, until the cops release the kitchen.'

'Don't go,' she said. She touched his hand. 'I need your support.'

'All right.' He reluctantly agreed. She was overpaying him, and he felt for her. 'But I'll only talk about building work. My story is you phoned me and I came straight over from my job on Woodgrange Road. You must tell them about finding the vandalism; don't bring me into it.'

'Agreed.'

'As an events manager, you must be used to problems.'

She threw up her hands. 'Aren't I just. Landowners, bands, toilets, oh don't talk to me about toilets, caterers, and complaining neighbours. I've had them all and more. I can sweet talk for England.'

He bet she could.

It wasn't the cops who came first, but the family.

Chapter 7

He and Judy had gone into the sitting room. It was one of two rooms at the front of the house, either side of the hallway. The other was the TV room. There was a sofa, two armchairs, bookshelves with a music centre on the lowest shelf, a fireplace with William Morris tiled surrounds, and a dark stained, very shiny dining table with six matching chairs, in its centre a dried flower display in a sturdy, ornate vase.

Jack had been reluctant to go in the room with his work boots, with its off-white fluffy carpet. Should he take them off? She waved away his reluctance, telling him to go in. Just as well, as he had a hole in his left sock which his big toe poked through.

The front door opened with excited voices.

'Maggie, Mo and Tom,' Judy said to him. 'Stay cool.'

She went out to greet her siblings, to bring them into the sitting room and prepare them for the devastation in the kitchen.

The three entered with Judy, two men and a woman. Jack, sitting on the sofa, stood up as they entered, and tried to work out who was who.

'Who is he?' said the woman. She had a short elfin cut, in jeans and T-shirt, clutching what must be the wedding dress to her already-showing pregnant abdomen.

Maggie, he thought. He could see the resemblance to Judy, same height, slightly turned-up nose. Though she was made up, purple lipstick, purple eyeliner and he could smell her scent from two yards away. Judy was lightly made up, if at all. No scent.

'This is Jack,' said Judy, pointing him out, 'he's a builder.'

'Why do we need a builder?'

'Sit down,' said Judy. 'We have a problem. Please, sit down.'

Jack stayed standing while the others settled themselves, frowning, wondering what was up. The man sitting next to Maggie on the sofa, that must be her fiance, Mo. He was Asian, quite dark brown, a little portly, in jeans and a yellow T-shirt, and smart Adidas trainers.

The other man, by elimination, had to be Tom, the brother. He was wearing a Peaky Blinders hat with curls coming out the front, green jeans, and a red silk scarf. Obviously dressing for effect.

'Hi, Jack,' he said, giving him a wave and a bright smile. 'I'm Tom, the clever one in the family, though they all think they are. Do you know, *the Joey bar leaps on to your tongue?*'

'Will you ever give it a rest,' exclaimed Maggie. 'Some dopy slogan for a chocolate bar he made up centuries ago, and he thinks he rules the world.'

'I will, honey, I will yet.'

'Forget stupid chocolate bars,' said Maggie. 'Our event organiser says there's a problem, Houston. And it needs a builder, so lay off the ad breaks.' She turned to Judy. 'It is not going to upset the wedding. Is it?'

'Come on, Judy,' said Mo. 'Tell us what's going on.'

She certainly had their attention. How was she going to deliver this? And what would their reaction be? He would keep quiet, speak only when he was spoken to. He was just the builder.

'The kitchen has been wrecked,' said Judy.

Maggie was instantly up, leaving the wedding dress on the sofa, rushing from the room, followed by the other two with cries of how, what, why, followed by Judy shouting, 'Don't go in. The police are coming. They said, don't go in!'

Jack stayed in the sitting room, listening to the cries from afar as they eyed the damage. A flurry of voices, all talking at once, coming from the end of the hallway. He could make out the odd word, but the volume told him what was going on. Shock, disbelief, bewilderment at the how and whys to their sanctum. Their magazine picture kitchen ripped to shreds.

He more or less knew what Judy was saying to them. Whether they were listening to her was moot, as they gazed at the smashed cupboards and shelves, the rivulets of broken china. He could imagine them, grouped at the door, pointing out this and that. How, who, why?

Maggie was the first back, closely followed by the others. Jack was seated on an arm of one of the armchairs. She came up close to him.

'Mr Builder!' she exclaimed, 'can you repair the kitchen by Saturday?'

'You have to phone the police!' shouted Tom at Judy.

'Shut up, shut up,' cried Maggie. 'This is more important than the cops. Please, builder, can you fix the kitchen by Saturday?'

'His name is Jack,' said Judy. 'Don't be so rude.'

They were grouped round him.

Maggie put an arm on his shoulder. 'I am so very sorry, Jack.' She tapped her stomach. 'Hormones. And the wedding is on Saturday. The reception here. I am a bundle of nerves. The caterers need the kitchen, everyone will come through to the marquee in the garden. Please say you can fix it by Saturday.'

'You must,' said Mo, pointing wildly. 'Or we can bring in a team. I'll pay!'

'Let's listen to the man, please,' said Tom. 'Jack, your chance to shine. Can you fix our kitchen?'

'Give me some space,' he said stretching his arms out. 'I feel a bit crushed.'

The ring backed off a pace.

'I've been here about half an hour,' said Jack, 'and I've got the picture.'

'Not difficult,' scowled Mo.

Jack ignored him. 'I realise the urgency. It's pretty basic. We have ordered replacement cupboards, shelves and fittings. They are coming tomorrow morning. I'll get them fitted by Friday at the latest.'

'Thank God,' exclaimed Maggie. 'You are a marvel.'

He noted how she had changed her tune, now that she needed him.

'I'll get going as soon as the police release the room,' he said.

'Due any minute,' said Judy. 'Coming with a forensic team. Shortly, whatever that means. That was 45 minutes ago.'

'I can't start,' said Jack, 'until they have gone. Hopefully this afternoon will be enough for them, and I can get moving in the morning. Clear up for a kick off. Take down the wrecked cupboards, and if the cupboards and shelves have come, begin fitting them.'

'We won't get in your way,' said Maggie. 'Will we, darling?'

Mo gave her a squeeze.

'I know you need the kitchen,' said Jack. 'But it's big enough for all of us. Once it's tidied up. Just keep out of my way, please.'

He knew it would be tricky working with people milling about. Though if one hat would rather they weren't there, the other wanted them chatting, and feeding him info.

'It will take two to lift those cupboards,' said Mo. 'Who is going to assist you?'

'I am,' said Judy.

The first Jack had heard of it. He did have a T-support which might suffice, but those cupboards were heavy. Probably could do it on his own, but it would be good to have Judy around. So maybe those barbells in her room would prove their utility.

'We also need to see what china has survived,' said Maggie.

'I'll be onto it as soon as the cops go,' said Judy. 'I'll make a list of what has to be done.'

'I cannot understand it,' exclaimed Tom. 'It makes no sense at all. Wrecking the kitchen. Why?'

'The police think it could be connected to Dad's murder,' said Judy.

'That is hooey!' said Mo. 'He was killed two months ago. Cliff confessed. It's all over bar the trial.'

'Cliff is innocent,' yelled Judy. 'How many times do I have to tell you! He was fitted up. Besides which, it has nothing to do with you, Mo. So butt out.'

Mo grimaced. Jack could feel his hatred of Judy.

'I apologise for my arrogant sister,' said Maggie to Jack, 'though I don't see why I should have to, but Mo happens to be my fiancé.' She had taken Mo's arm. 'And will be part of the family on Saturday.'

'I don't believe Cliff did it,' said Tom.

'So who did?' said Mo.

Jack realised this was a regular family bout. Judy and Tom in the red corner, Mo in the blue and Maggie hopping back and forth. No ref, it was one of those scraps where everyone is in the ring slugging it out.

The doorbell rang.

Chapter 8

Judy went to the door. The others stayed where they were. Out of the window, a police car could be seen and, behind it, a forensic van.

'They took over the house, last time they were here,' said Maggie to Jack, who was now her best friend. 'Two months ago, our dad was murdered, as you may have gathered.'

He had already gathered more than that.

'Went through everything in my room,' said Tom. 'I kept looking for things for a month.'

'Just the kitchen this time,' said Mo. 'And no one is dead. I'm just surprised they've come mob handed. We had a burglary at my place couple of years back.' He flapped his hands. 'Nobody came. Too small to bother with.'

Two police officers in plain clothes appeared at the sitting room door. Jack knew them both. His school friend DI Fayyad Kamani, and his sidekick, DS Nova Taylor. It had to be her. Both smartly dressed in navy blue suits. Fayyad insisted on it. They were not hippies, he'd told Jack.

'Good morning, everyone,' said Fayyad. 'I am Detective Inspector Fayyad Kamani.'

'We well remember,' said Maggie. 'And she's your sergeant.'

'Detective sergeant,' said Nova. 'We are here to look at your kitchen, which, we have been informed, has been vandalised.'

'And how,' said Maggie. 'Just days from our wedding.' She clutched Mo's hand.

Jack thought, maybe that could be thrown in as a complication. To take any heat off Judy. Someone, for whatever reason, wanting to sabotage the wedding. Maggie would take that on board, if no one else.

'Hello, Jack,' said Nova.

'Hello,' he said. Ice cold.

The last time they had spoken was in the Himalaya last night. Seemed a lifetime ago. He'd walked out after she told him that she was seeing someone. She'd called after him, but what was there left to say?

Jack wanted to leave, with Nova here, but he'd said he'd support Judy. A mistake, he should have gone. Though it was as well to know what Judy was saying, his partner in crime. He being the junior partner, but if it got out, the cops might not see it that way.

The detectives left, on their way to the kitchen. He could hear them talking as they walked down the hallway.

'The same cops who investigated the murder,' said Maggie.

'They think there might be a connection,' said Tom.

'Hooey,' said Mo. 'And I don't care what Judy says. They've got the killer.'

'I wish you wouldn't say that,' said Maggie.

'Sorry, sweetheart,' he said and put his arm round her.

'Why should someone smash up the kitchen?' said Tom. 'I keep thinking of that. The stupidity of it.'

He still had his Peaky Blinders hat on, though it was tipped a little further back, showing more of his curls.

'Someone who wants us to leave,' said Maggie. 'It can be so snooty, this road. Some of them think they are in Buck-ingham Palace.'

She rose, taking her wedding dress, and placing it care-fully over the back of one of the dining table chairs.

'Or someone who wants to sabotage your wedding,' said Jack.

Might as well throw that in as a smokescreen.

'Do you really think so?' said Maggie, her hands clutching at her cheeks at the very idea.

'Perhaps someone is trying to tell us the cops arrested the wrong person,' said Tom.

Mo threw up his hands.

'And how exactly does smashing the kitchen do that, Mr Adman!'

Tom shrugged. Jack had the feeling he enjoyed winding Mo up. Not that it was difficult. Maggie came over to Jack.

'This is a fraught time, Jack. You have to excuse us.'

'Of course,' he said. 'Are you working?'

'I'm a singer songwriter,' she said. 'I do gigs here and there. Judy gives me a spot every so often, at her events.'

'She is brilliant,' exclaimed Mo.

'He's biased,' said Maggie. 'Take no notice.'

'She is good,' said Tom. 'She did a jingle for the agency.'

Maggie blew a raspberry. 'Lots of cash for next to nothing.'

'It's why I am there, honey.'

'She's doing a couple of songs at the wedding,' said Mo.

'Don't tell everyone,' exclaimed Maggie. 'It's meant to be a surprise.'

'He's not coming,' said Mo. And turning to Jack, added 'No offence.'

'None taken.'

He was aware how the kitchen destruction had excited everyone. They were talkative, which gave him a fuller picture of the family, and had raised his status, so he could ask questions. He was Maggie's best pal, so OK by Mo too. And Tom liked everyone. Could one of these nice people have killed Richard Ffrench?

Nova came in. Or should he now call her Detective Sergeant Nova Taylor, as she was a cop now and just a cop as far as he was concerned.

'Can we talk, Jack?'

She beckoned him to follow her.

'She fancies you,' said Maggie quietly, with a smirk.

If only, thought Jack, and followed her into the hallway. They went into the TV room opposite. He was shaky in her presence, though he doubted this chat would be anything personal. She was strictly DS Taylor.

There was a massive TV set dominating the room, a music amplifier on its own table nearby, the speakers either side of the TV. A large sofa faced the TV, with two armchairs, all facing the one-eyed monster. There were long drapes on the window as in the sitting room. Behind the sofa was a baby-grand piano, with a guitar leaning against it. Most likely Maggie practised here. And the family watched TV together when they weren't quarrelling. Though he'd noted there was another TV set in the kitchen, should the conflict get unbearable.

Nova sat on the arm of the sofa. Jack took the arm of an armchair. He didn't want to get comfortable as he had half an idea what this would be about.

'I'm not going to talk about last night,' she said.

'Good,' he said.

'Some other time for that.'

He shrugged. Not wanting to give any hint of his hurt. She was imposing, strong, a black belt in judo. Desire stirred, mid helplessness. Quell self pity, said Max. So easily said. He was like a hollow statue, paper thin, a touch and he'd collapse.

She continued. 'You are here as a builder, Jack.' He said nothing, he knew where this was going, how could it not. He loved and hated her. But this was police business, strictly.

'But less than two hours ago,' Nova went on, 'Judy phoned the station asking for a reference for you as a private detective.'

Here it comes.

'It's obvious why,' she said. 'She believes Cliff Ffrench, her twin, to be innocent of their father's murder. She has told us that repeatedly. And of course, she is entitled to bring in a private investigator. But she wants you here as a builder too. I see how that works. You work in the kitchen as a builder, chat to everyone as they come in for breakfast and so forth. And they don't know you are undercover.'

She was getting there, step by step. A canny soul was Nova. Damn her in her smart suit and pony tail. The hot cop, while he shivered as if the armchair he was on was made of ice.

'I was here two months ago, Jack, investigating the murder of Richard Ffrench. And I can tell you, this house was in perfect repair then. So what was there for a builder to do?'

He said nothing. Always a wise choice. Not give away his need, or how she was homing in.

'So, I believe, work was made for you. How else could you be undercover?' She stared at him. The silent treatment, to get him to speak in the uncomfortable pause. Knowing this technique, he looked down, at the carpet and her polished black shoes.

Aeons passed, until she spoke again.

'I want to see your phone please, Jack. Your recent calls.'

He looked up, Nova was holding out her hand. He could refuse, and contemplated doing so. But she'd get it in the end. It wouldn't work if he held back because of animosity. Where would that get him?

A night in the cells for obstructing justice? With his phone taken anyway.

With reluctance, Jack took out his phone, and slowly, with deliberation, as if he didn't care, flipped to calls, looked down the list, and handed over the phone.

Let's see how smart you are. How I have fouled up.

Nova looked at the calls on the screen for perhaps a minute. Her face twisting as she calculated. She then took a picture of the calls page with her own phone, and handed his back.

'You had a call with Judy just over an hour ago,' she said.

He nodded. It was the call they had set up to fool the cops. This was its test.

'She phoned to tell me her kitchen had been vandalised,' he said. 'And asked me if I could come over right away? I was just working up the road, so I came. What's the problem?'

Jack knew very well what the problem was, even as he lied. But he had a tale to stick to. He was, after all, the living lie, hiding his feelings for her, hiding the truth of the kitchen vandalism.

'Let me be clear, Jack. I think you and Judy have concocted a tale. One of you smashed up the kitchen, or perhaps both of you.'

'That's crazy,' he said, knowing it wasn't at all.

'Please leave your toolbox here, Jack, when you leave.'

This was one he hadn't expected. Though he should have. This woman was destined to do the dirty on him, one way or another.

'I need the tools for my job on the high street,' he protested.

'We need them too. A crime has been committed, and we need to eliminate you as a perpetrator.'

He bit back a curse. This was serious. She had almost got it. Her error was suggesting that he and Judy had both smashed up the kitchen. When, in fact, he was stuck outside the locked kitchen door while Judy hammered away. If the cops had them as a team, and a jury took that on board, it would mean jail for sure. In cahoots for an insurance fraud and making work for his investigation.

'I'm not happy leaving my tools here,' he said. 'You know I need them.' Hoping in vain for some softness from this woman he had been with for two years. 'And I certainly did not smash up the kitchen.'

'I hope that is true, Jack,' she said. 'Sincerely. I am sorry to put you through this, but I am a detective.'

Always a problem in their relationship.

He rose. 'Have we done?'

'We have. For now.'

'Thank you, DS Taylor.'

Jack left the room, his stomach aching as if after a low blow. Could she find anything against him in his toolbox? It had been open while Judy was on the rampage with his hammer. He had cleaned out chippings, but there could well be the odd wood splinter, china dust.

All he could say to that was that he had looked around the kitchen, after he was called over, opened his toolbox, measured up or whatever. Yes, it was a crime scene, but he did have work to do. Something like that. He needed to talk to Judy, make sure their tales tallied.

He went into the sitting room. The others were seated, including Judy. No doubt wondering why he'd been called out, and discussing the options.

'What was that about?' said Judy.

He thought of lying for the benefit of Maggie, Mo and Tom, but why bother?

'She thinks I smashed up the kitchen,' he said.

'That is ridiculous,' declared Judy.

'What rubbish,' said Maggie. 'Stupid cop.'

'They are keeping my toolbox as evidence.' He sighed. 'They might find some china chippings in it, a splinter or two, while I was measuring up.' That was for Judy's benefit. 'But I've got to go. Work to do. I must sort out my other tools. What a shambles!'

At the sitting room door, he turned. 'See you tomorrow. Let's hope the cops are out of our hair.'

'I'll see you out,' said Judy.

Once out the front door, along the path, safely out of earshot, she said, 'She thinks it was *you* smashed up the kitchen?'

'Or maybe the two of us in cahoots.'

'How did she work that out?'

Jack shrugged. 'Oh, she's a clever one. You asked her to give me a reference as a detective. Then she comes here and finds I am employed as a builder.'

'With no building work.' Judy nodded, now in the picture.

'So some was made by you, by me or by both of us.'

Judy blew out her cheeks.

'I am so sorry, I got you into this.'

Me too, he might have added, but didn't. Too late for such regrets. His hurt quotient could hardly be higher.

'I'll see you tomorrow,' he said, 'assuming the cops have gone.'

And left.

Chapter 9

The sun was shining as Jack walked along Osborne Road, only too glad to be out of that zoo. Not only had Nova dumped him, she was accusing him of vandalism, which would be paid for by insurance. And so fraud in addition. The woman he had gone out with for two years had turned on him. 'I am a detective,' she had said. So that entitled her to slap him in handcuffs and get him banged up for two years.

Perhaps he'd ask the judge if he could go to Pentonville. There, he could talk to Cliff, maybe he'd be in the same cell. Work out his innocence or guilt, if Cliff talked in his sleep.

He hoped he was exaggerating Nova's desire to pursue him to the ends of the earth. In his anger and hurt, he could imagine doing the same to her. But detective she may be, his guilt had not been proved. And if he were charged, Judy would get them the smartest lawyer in the kingdom. Though clearly that wasn't working for Cliff, who was banged up awaiting trial, the police believing they had enough evidence to prove him guilty of his father's murder. Admittedly, a confession was not a great help, even to a top lawyer fighting his case.

That was one unlucky house. First the father is murdered, then one of the sons is arrested for his murder, framed insisted Judy, and now he and she could be arrested too.

Back home, he made a simple lunch. Cheese and tomato sandwich and a cup of tea, that filled a hole. Thinking all the time about Nova's accusation. He and Judy were claiming some person unknown had got into the house, must've had a key as there was no sign of a break in, and smashed up the kitchen. Nova was saying that was too far fetched to be believable. Judy and Jack had done it. Which they were claiming was ridiculous. Both scenarios far fetched in their way. But slightly less so was the one saying he or Judy, or both had done it. They were after all real people, and any vandal was unknown with an unknown motive.

And a phantom of Judy's and his imagination.

Jack kept his more valuable tools in the house, like drills, but the rest with another toolbox was in his van outside the house. He took a drill from the house as he left, and a toolbox out of the van, he'd do some work for Dobbs this afternoon, putting in the drill and bits he brought down from his flat, two saws, chisels, screws and whatever else he could think of. There was bound to be something he hadn't.

He stopped and thought about what he was doing. He couldn't park on the high street, but why not park at the end of Osborne Road, which was close by where he was working in both places. And if he forgot anything at Dobbs', he could go out to the van and get it.

He drove to Osborne Road, parked and alighted with his toolbox. He greeted the Patels as he came through the stationery shop. He was in no mood for a chat. And went upstairs. There, he spent an hour taking up rotten floorboards. Not all of them, just the worst. It was a depressing place, bleak and dusty, bringing out his loneliness and Nova's bashing of him. As if her thinking was to keep on kicking him, then he'll know there is no chance whatsoever of resurrecting their relationship. She was out to make him hate her.

Her plan probably didn't exist, it was him making himself too important. The centre of a tragedy. He wasn't dead, almost felt it, wished it. Keep sawing, pulling up boards. Don't hit the bottle.

Misery feeds on misery.

The rotten floorboards, the ones taken out, he'd piled against the wall, feeling a sympathy for them. Done with, discarded, no appreciation of their years of faithful use, like old servants, sick and ailing, kicked out after a lifetime of service.

Kick out self pity, said Max.

Got you, man. I will attempt to stand up.

Dobbs had to buy replacement boards. Not himself, he didn't trust Dobbs anyway as he hadn't had a penny from him. He needed to contact him, send him an invoice. Get some money out of him to compensate for this dreadful workplace.

As luck would have it, Dobbs came up.

'Not much going on here,' he said in his blustery East End accent.

He was in his 50s, grey haired, what was left of it, quite fat, in a baggy grey suit. A landlord, with quite a few properties, he wouldn't say how many, this would be just another in his portfolio.

'I need you to buy replacement floorboards,' said Jack.

'You get them and I'll repay you.'

'No way,' said Jack. 'I haven't had a penny from you. I need floorboards, wood sealant, paint and plaster, and glass for the window in the bedroom. I'll make you a list, and you get the materials.'

'You get it, Jack. I'll repay you.'

'Where have I heard that before?'

Jack began packing his tools.'

'What are you doing?'

'I am packing up,' he said. 'I've been working here for nothing. And this is an end of it.'

'Buy what you need and I'll repay you for it, and for the work you've done so far.'

'I had a feeling about the job from the off,' said Jack. 'I asked you for half payment and all I got was promises. I'd be a mug working here any longer.'

He hefted his tool box and went to the door.

'You can't leave a job half done!' Mr Dobbs called after him as he went down the stairs.

Jack ignored the irate landlord, his ex-client. This was where he'd been his most miserable, that morning he'd been planning to get drunk, fortunately or unfortunately, interrupted by Judy. He felt energised getting out of there. So he'd lost money, but boy was it a win to walk out.

He walked through the shop, saying goodbye to the Patels, went out the shop door into the street, crossed the road, loaded up his van and drove home.

Good riddance to Dobbs.

As he came into his house with just the drill, the toolbox left in the van for the morning, he noted the bicycle in the small foyer. There were two doors for the two flats, one for the old lady who had the downstairs flat, and the other for his, the upstairs flat. His daughter was now cycling every-where and she was obviously in. He had put in some large hooks so she could hang up her bike, so it would take up minimal space in their small foyer.

Jack unlocked the flat door. Mia's cycle helmet was on the bottom step. Some pleasant company anyway, no cops on his case or grasping landlords who expected you to work for nothing.

He was broke. That matched his mood. Just an engage-ment ring, he would have to take back, and hope they would redeem. Judy, he recalled, was due to pay him half the money for building and detective work. And how he needed it, now he'd given Dobbs the heave-ho.

Mia was at the table reading a book, her laptop open, as he entered.

His daughter was almost as tall as he was, slim, a mass of dark brown curly hair, occasionally tidy. In faded jeans, not pre-faded but genuinely worn out. She despised those torn at the knee. Why destroy good clothes? Mia lived half with him and half with his ex wife, her mother, Alison. Coming and going as she liked, Alison having a house just a mile away.

'You're back early,' she said.

'So are you.'

'Private study. I thought I could work here as you were out on a job. Mum's got a plumber in.'

'I walked out on Dobbs,' he said. 'The job upstairs the stationers on Woodgrange Road. Couldn't get any money out of him, so I walked, with him yelling after me. I felt like I'd won the battle of Waterloo.'

'He must owe you money.'

'He does. And I am not going to get it. More fool me. I should've insisted on half up front.' He put a hand up to stop her. 'I know. Stupid of me.' He appealed. 'You wouldn't like to make a cuppa for your old Dad?'

'Don't give me that 'old' malarkey,' she said. 'I've seen you running up ladders and carting paving slabs. Though you are in luck, I could do with a break myself.'

She rose and headed for the kitchen.

'You make the next,' she said, going in.

'Promise.'

He felt better, appreciated. Self pity was just misery piled on misery, as Max might have said. Probably did. Max ran the sessions at Alcohol Halt for alcoholics and substance abusers. He hadn't been a while, should go back as he needed support.

Jack took down his laptop from a nearby shelf, sat at the table and loaded it up, wondering how close he was to his overdraft limit. While the machine was going through its welcomes, he had a peek at the book Mia was reading. A school library book. On the open page were two photos of a glacier, one twenty years ago, a river of ice from the mountain top to the bottom of the photo, while the second was the same place, with just a little ice at the summit. Peru, in the Andes.

Mia was doing environmental studies which fitted with her doomy view of human progress. No matter how he might counter with wind turbines, recycling and solar panels, she would top him with loss of ice in the Arctic ocean, and methane steaming off the tundra. He sometimes felt he could do environmental studies himself, having picked up the syllabus from his daughter.

Jack went to his bank page, putting in the codes, and his mother's maiden name which reminded him, he must go and see her. Though he found her somewhat boring, lecturing him on his mortal soul, while watching some daytime soap. Mia cycled there, to her block of flats near Plaistow station, much more often than he did, dropping in for half an hour to get a cup of tea and biscuits from her granny, while they lectured each other about the end of days. Both had a different take on it but agreed it was coming.

'Yes!' He threw up his arms in triumph.

A thousand quid had come in from Judy, half upfront as he'd asked. Great to have a good payer, someone he didn't have to chase, but boy didn't she owe him. And two fifty had come in, from that roofing job he'd almost forgotten about. He was solvent.

Screw Dobbs.

Mia came in with a tray, with two mugs of tea and some toast.

'We should get some marmalade,' she said, giving him a mug, and putting the plate of toast between them. 'I heard a whoop of triumph,' she added. 'Have you solved a crime? That woman who phoned this morning, she woke me up. Said she couldn't get through to you, so I told her where you were working. You really should keep your phone on. If you want work.'

He didn't want to go through his miseries and say why the phone had been off.

'Bad habit,' he said.

Mia had been a partner in Forest Gate Investigations, but it couldn't pay her. Though she did some online research for him and he paid her when he himself got paid for the occasional detective work.

'Thanks for passing on the address,' he said. 'She came up to see me. We went to Costa, and she told me what she wanted. And she's given me half the cash upfront. No messing.'

'What's the job?'

Jack wondered how much to tell her. Though Mia was reliable, good at keeping confidential information to herself, and a good sounding board. And he might need her help.

'Her name is Judy Ffrench, two fs,' he said. 'And her brother Cliff Ffrench is in jail, awaiting trial for murdering their father. But she claims he's innocent.'

'And you have to prove it. If you can, Sherlock.'

He ignored the dig. 'She lives in one of those double-fronted houses on Osborne Road. The family has oodles of cash.'

'Forest Gate Festival is on Osborne Road. On Saturday.'

'They are having a wedding that day. Not Judy, but her sister Maggie.'

'We've a stall at the Festival,' said Mia. 'Forest Gate Carbon Sinks. We will have three butler sinks. One with reusable plastic in, a second with recyclable plastic and the last with single-use junk. Too easy to get the junk, all those dreadful tetrapaks and junk food boxes. On the day itself, we'll send off kids through the festival to get us stuff to fill the sinks and to earn a Carbon Sink badge.'

'The organisers will love you, cleaning up for them.'

'And oh yes, before I forget, Mum's having a dinner party Friday night and invites you and Nova.'

Here it comes. Ah well, couldn't be avoided. He took a deep breath.

'Me and Nova have split up.'

'Again!'

'This is it. The end. She has someone else.'

He considered saying he'd proposed to Nova and been rejected. But no. She didn't have to know.

'Sorry to hear you've split up,' said Mia. 'I didn't like her at first. A cop. Too much trouble with them on demos. But I got to like her.' She stopped, realising she was talking about herself. 'Are you cut up?'

'I am.' She'd asked. He had to admit it. 'She broke it off.'

'I am so sorry, Dad.'

'Tell your mum thanks, but I am not feeling very sociable.'

They didn't speak a while. Jack sent an invoice to Dobbs, not expecting payment, but could threaten him with small claims court. Might work. Mia had opened her laptop and was writing, every so often consulting the book.

For dinner, Jack feeling flush, Mia ordered on his credit card a take out from Moon House, a nearby Chinese takeaway. While eating, they talked about her school courses. She was 18 and had taken a year off before this one, unsure what to do, finally deciding to go back to school. Her final year was after the summer holidays, beginning at the end of next week. The environmental science teacher was great, she said, and she'd made good friends on the course, all into saving the planet from fossil fuel maniacs.

She was looking at University prospectuses. Unsure whether to stay in London or get away. Much of the climate action was in London, though it would be good to get away from her parents. No offence.

None taken. Though he'd miss her if she left town. She'd be back for the holidays but it wasn't the same, her dropping round like this. But he had to accept it was her life and she would go her own way.

They had just finished eating when the doorbell rang.

Mia went down, and came back with Judy who was wearing a pink silk scarf and a light red jacket.

'Your client,' said Mia.

Jack introduced them, and he and Judy went into the kitchen, leaving Mia to her school work. At her laptop, earplugs in, writing an essay about the effect of glacier loss on local populations. She had pushed away the remnants of the takeaway, to be dealt with later.

The habit of the household.

It was a little awkward in the kitchen. Judy wore more make up than earlier in the day and a haunting perfume, which made him think this might not just be a business call. Not that he was averse, but Mia being here made it tricky.

'I thought we needed to chat,' she said.

They were seated at the kitchen table. Dirty crockery was piled in the sink, but the table was clear. He offered her tea, but she declined.

'DS Taylor suspects us,' she said.

He noted the 'us'. How he had been roped in. She had smashed up the cupboards and shelves. He had gone along with it for the money. He could have refused, but now that he'd taken her cash, me had become us.

'Taylor has no proof,' he said. 'Our story is you came back from your walk, and found the kitchen smashed up. You phoned the cops, then me. I came over. And that is it. Stick to that scenario. Tell them I did a bit of measuring up, which would account for any china chippings or wood splinters in my toolbox.'

'Keep it simple. I agree. I came home, and found the kitchen vandalised. Then phoned the cops and then you. Got it.'

'Except you had asked Nova for a reference for me as a detective.'

'A bit of bad luck there,' she said. 'She deduced work had to be made for you, so you could investigate undercover.'

'She's sussed us.'

Judy nodded. 'But she can't prove it. Let's stick to our tale. The unknown vandal. Hold fast. I will take up your offer of tea.'

He rose and filled the kettle.

'Tell me about the chain of pharmacies,' he said. 'How is the ownership made up?'

He tried to relax, she was attractive and this was a close space. Her perfume. Just make tea. He got the teapot and mugs ready. Just tea, no biscuits, as he didn't know she was coming. And quell those fantasies.

'There are 12 pharmacies making up Ffrenchco. Spread over the East End.'

He was leaning against the worktop, needing the space. Hers was a foxy delivery. The words prosaic, but he couldn't help watching her very red lips as she spoke. You don't put that on for a visit. Or do you? A woman he'd known wouldn't go out without make-up.

Half hearing. She was employing him. Don't blow it by making a pass.

'Uncle Alec has 10% of the shares,' she went on. 'He's the overall manager. He's an old friend of Dad's, been working together 40 years. He's not an uncle really, we just call him that. He's had those shares forever. Dad had the rest. We had no share in the business until he died, and his will handed us our shares. There's Lily, our housekeeper, she got 5%. And his four children, that's me, Tom, Maggie and Cliff have the other 85% between us. Though Cliff loses his share if he's found guilty and me, Maggie and Tom, take it over. We've also inherited the house between us, plus Dad's various investments.'

Was she out of his league? Though she had only recently become rich, or well off, as how rich is rich? Her father's death was only two months ago. She'd soon picked up the habits of the wealthy. Smashing perfectly good cupboards. Paying over the top for a private investigator.

'Lily, your housekeeper, has 5%,' he'd heard that much. 'A little odd,' he said, trying not to look at her as if she might read his thoughts.

'It is. Though the will states she must keep working for us till she's 65 to keep her shares. She's 53 now, so 12 more years. Lily just does a couple of hours in the mornings, 8 to 10 am. She was sleeping with Dad. They thought it was a secret, but we all knew it. She'd come over to the house at 6 am, sleep with him for two hours, then do the housework. I caught her once, coming out of his room and wiping her make up off. We weren't suppose to know our father was having it off with the housekeeper, but you can't keep that secret. We pretended to him we didn't know.'

Jack was paying a little heed, enough to be seen to be listening. But he'd fail the exam. He'd have to pick this up again tomorrow. Wondering what might happen if he tried to kiss her. She was employing him. Good money. It would not do to get it wrong. Make like you are paying attention. Listen.

He'd missed some but caught the tail end.

'That's why she got her 5%,' he said, hoping he'd caught it correctly. 'More than a housekeeper. What's it worth, moneywise?'

Judy bit her lip, thinking. 'I'd say around fifteen thou a year. She also gets 10 thou per annum for housekeeping, plus extra for any specials. Like, she's getting £500 for managing the wedding catering. She does alright, does Lily. Owns a flat within walking distance. We think Dad bought it for her. Not absolutely sure. Neither of them said so, but we got the feeling. Too expensive for her on her own.'

This was not the best place to gather info, not in such close proximity. Her kitchen maybe, but not one this size. He couldn't concentrate.

Jack placed the teapot on the table, two mugs and a milk jug. Oat milk, Mia wouldn't have cow's milk, said it was tainted with the blood of slaughtered calves. He sat down, thighs touching. Neither moving away. Maybe he was being too careful.

Dare he hold her hand?

'Change was in the wind,' she said. 'Dad was talking to his lawyer. It had to be that he was making a new will. He didn't like Mo, wouldn't let him in the house, so Maggie may well have got nothing. Tom's free living annoyed him, so he'd be deleted. Dad was racist and homophobic. I might have squeaked through, but I'd left home, which might have given me the chop. I couldn't take any more of his foibles.'

Keep your hands to yourself, he thought. You are a private investigator, or should be.

'How might Cliff have fared in any new will?' he said, an investigator question, not a sex obsessed man who had just been dumped.

'Dad didn't like his lifestyle. Cliff's an artist and Dad was not into art. He might've liked it more if Cliff was successful but he was definitely in the poor house. That's why he was still living at home, having to take Dad's jibes. I gave Cliff work every so often at events I was organising, running art workshops and such like, but that was pretty occasional.'

How could he think this way and take anything in? Half listening, a skill he had some practice in. Were women that different?

'Does this draft will exist or was it all talk?' he said, sounding so sensible.

'It exists all right,' she said. 'His solicitor said so, but wouldn't let me see it. Gave me some legal nonsense. Stuffy old man.'

'The police might have it,' he said. 'When it's murder, the solicitor can't say no to the cops.'

She gave a wry smile. 'We are not exactly top of the class when it comes to the police.'

'I'll have a go.'

And then, out of nowhere, she kissed him. It shouldn't have been a surprise, but the signals had seemed to cancel each other out until he'd reckoned this was a business meeting, not realising she was thinking much the same as he was.

Lips melded, talk of draft wills and cops jettisoned. An enduring embrace, washing away Nova the cop, Nova the lover, Nova anything anywhere, Dobbs and the troubles of the world. Warm, soft and liquid. An enveloping illusion. Or the only reality.

A drip of eternity.

There was a rap on the door. They broke apart. She wiped his mouth with her sleeve.

'Come in,' he said, separating like guilty teenagers.

Mia opened the door cautiously, her laptop and book under her arm.

'I'm sure you two still have lots to talk about. I'm going home.'

Chapter 10

Judy didn't stay much longer. Mia had broken the mood. And an affair, Judy told him, quite sensibly, might make them careless and get them arrested. Let things cool down. His common sense agreed, his body didn't. That was some kiss. How he had lapped up the warmth. But he didn't quite trust her. Judy, attractive and rich, could pick and choose, and if they ever got started, she could dump him soon enough, and he could do without that, even as he regretted her leaving.

Jack was simply there, convenient. Or inconvenient considering the kitchen shenanigans. An event organiser, he suspected, could get the pick of the crop, and move on to the next event. He imagined her with a clipboard, negotiating, bands down the list sucking up to her. He was too vulnerable, the hurt after Nova, but he would have taken Judy. Of course he would. Ace mug.

Unable to sleep, the night was too long, two alpha women tossing him between them. And he couldn't get free. One was employing him, the other investigating him.

The high of the kiss dropped him into a chasm of despair. The early hours were worse. If he could get through them, to dawn, to sunlight, to work. Sawing and drilling drove away his demon. Noise and sawdust. It had been good that Mia dropped round, he always enjoyed their chats. She'd be off to university, quite likely out of London, but still another year at school.

He must stay sober. The garage on the Romford Road was open 24 hours. He could drown the two women in whisky, drown himself too. And make work tomorrow impossible.

No solution to anything, Max said.

Clever, clever Max. A bit sickening sometimes, but always right.

At two thirty in the morning, Jack got out of bed, dressed, gathered up his telescope and the mount, and carried them out to his van.

He set off, driving to the car park on Wanstead Flats, about a mile away. The streets were quiet, sensible people in bed, the shops shuttered, Forest Gate station closed. The street well lit, a light on here and there in the flats above the shops. Quarrelling lovers or insomniacs, alkies pickling their brains, or druggies passing the pipe, not caring whether it was day or night. A mother awake with a fractious child.

Hardly any traffic.

Jack was a regular on the Flats at night. Nova would come from time to time, the telescope sessions bonding them. Mia too. Though not this late. But if he'd have stayed at home, he'd have given in to the demon.

At the empty car park, he unloaded the wheelbarrow, the telescope and mount. He carefully placed them in the wheelbarrow, locked the van and headed off into the gloom of the Flats. Now he had some cash, he should buy a power-pack for the scope. Then with his phone and the right app, the telescope would find any particular star or planet. Like magic. But it always struck him as cheating. He knew the heavens pretty well. It was just the planets that wandered, and a glance at his astronomy mag would tell him what was where any night.

There was a half moon, the old faithful. Pity Mia wasn't here, she knew many of the craters, delighted in their searches. There was no one about. He felt a little heroic, for daring to be here at all. He was free. Not even Nova could get him out here.

Dark, shadowy, trees were just visible as black on black, street lights at the far fringes, as he pushed on with the wheelbarrow. Light pollution was unavoidable in the city, but he had a favourite site, right in the centre of the Flats, as far away from lights as he could get.

While setting up the scope, he thought about Judy's visit. She was attractive, no doubt about that, but at the same time bossy. And he hated being ordered about. It was why he worked on his own. No gaffer. But clients could be difficult. And she was one, paying over the odds, and getting him in trouble.

There was a moment when he could have walked away. When she had just smashed the cupboards and opened the kitchen door to let him in. It was then. He could have said, I am not doing this. He had almost cried at the sight of those destroyed cabinets. Solid oak, splintered and shattered, that hit his heart, the sight of the ruin. All the work that had gone into them. They were topnotch. Just as well, he hadn't told Mia. She'd have gone bananas. Going on and on, about the waste, about all that carbon going into landfill, about the pointless stupidity.

And how could he argue?

Judy had assuaged his hurt with money. Two thousand, half now. And she had paid up quickly, knowing once he had taken it, she had him. Could he yet back out? Split on her, and get off himself.

That could rebound. She might counter-blame him, and then where would they be? The cupboards were smashed beyond repair. Turning on Judy wouldn't heal them. He must stick with his lies, and support hers.

The moon was quite high in the sky. The terminator well placed, that line between light and dark on the moon, that threw shadows in the craters it crossed, making them more visible and dramatic. The terminator made him think of Arnold Schwarzenegger, who had lived in Forest Gate in the late 60s, and had trained in a local gym to be Mr Universe. He was in the film, *The Terminator*, a killing machine disguised as a human, destroying anyone in his way.

That brought him back to Judy, the Terminator, destroyer of cupboards, smashing any in her way. Could he salvage them? Be the hero in his own B movie.

Jack had a thought that would make life more liveable. He must get to the house early, before she wakes up and takes over.

His telescope was centred on the Apennines, a row of mountains just up from the centre of the moon, easy to find. He stayed there awhile, then straying to the nearby crater Archimedes, admiring its beautiful circle of cliffs, a kilometre high, and then heading further off to Plato. Old pals who would never betray him.

The terminator crossing them without destruction.

Chapter 11

Jack drove to the house, arriving there by 7.30. He'd meant to be there at 6.30. Some hope, considering how little sleep he'd got. Coming back from the Flats, it still took him some time to get to sleep. His alarm had gone off at six, and he'd switched it off, sleeping on for another hour. He leapt out of bed, quick wash, and out.

He stopped at the Co-op for a coffee and two croissants, and consumed them at the top of Osborne Road, thinking he'd get little at the house, considering the blitzed kitchen. His good intentions were to be first on the job. So he could take charge.

Refuelled with the croissants and caffeine hit, he drove to the house. Once parked, Jack took his toolbox out of the van, walked up the path and rang the bell.

The sound echoed through the wide hallway.

The door opened. It was Mo, Maggie's fiance. Suited, obviously ready for work, a strong smell of aftershave.

'Bright and early, good for you,' said Mo, tapping him on the shoulder as if they were old friends. 'Fix that kitchen, mate. We are depending on you, me and Maggie. Has to be pukka for the wedding on Saturday.'

'Have the cops gone?'

'Yes,' said Mo. 'The CSI people left late last night. It's ours again, with all the mess. Who on earth could have done such a thing?'

'Some crazy person,' he said, with a vision of Judy wielding his hammer. She had been crazy, so no lie.

'Must go. Work calls. The kitchen is impossible, like a bomb hit it. I'll get some breakfast on the way in. Get that kitchen done, mate, and we'll love you forever.'

With a wave, Mo strode off down the path. Good to be in demand. He'd best deliver. Jack went in, closing the front door, going down the hallway to the kitchen. A middle aged woman was in there, motionless amidst the debris, helpless in indecision. Nothing had been done, as Mo had indicated. Just as well, as he had plans.

That had to be Lily. She was short, a little plump, with red curly hair, quite buxom, wearing jeans, a loose blue top, an apron, and tennis shoes. Set for work but bewildered.

'I'm Jack,' he said. 'The builder. Come to put this right.'

'This is terrible.' Her hands held her face. 'A calamity. How did it happen? I've just got here. I was going to put coffee on, but I can't. Not with all this.' She swung her arms round at the debris. 'I can't believe it.'

'Someone broke in,' he said.

'Why?' She was mesmerized by the destruction.

'I don't know.'

He did of course. The Terminator did it. To make work for him. Almost a comedy, but all that good oak splintered and shattered. It hit him again. What a waste.

'Get us a couple of brooms,' he said. 'We'll get the stuff on the floor onto the patio, and make some working space.'

'I don't know what's going on in this house,' she said. 'First Mr Ffrench is murdered by his son. Calls himself an artist, the lowlife. And now this. All his kids, I tell you, they never respected him. Just me. I made him happy. And was I appreciated?' She waved her hands as if trying to rid herself of the horror.

He would have liked to have known more about her lack of appreciation, but she said no more, rendered silent by all the work to be done.

'Get the brooms,' he repeated. 'We'll make a start.'

She nodded, grateful to be told what to do, and left.

Jack took out a pair of rough leather gloves from his tool-box, and put them on. The kitchen garden door had a key in the lock on the inside. Not good practice, he thought. They could at least put it on a shelf.

He opened the garden door and began carrying larger pieces of wood to the patio. It would have to go out the front, but the patio would do for now.

Judy came into the kitchen, sans make up, or so little it didn't show. She wore jeans, an old T-shirt and trainers, her hair tied back in a ponytail. Ready for work.

'We'll order a skip,' she said, in event organiser mode. 'To take all the debris away, the broken china, smashed cupboards, throw them all in. Off it all goes. And we are all set to fit the replacements.'

'No,' he said.

She stared at him, knowing exactly what had to be done.

'Excuse me, Jack. I'm not sure what cloud you are on this morning. What else should be done with the rubbish?'

'If it goes into a skip, it will end up in landfill.'

She shrugged. 'That's not our problem, Jack. We have to get moving pronto on the kitchen.'

Which she had destroyed.

'In landfill, the wood will rot,' he said. 'In the absence of oxygen forming methane which is 30 time a more powerful climate gas than carbon dioxide.'

A direct quote from Mia. Like water wearing away rock, his daughter had got through to him. She had explained, in words of one syllable, why landfill was a bad choice for organic material. And putting the book down in front of him and pointing out the paragraphs.

'So what do you think we should do?' she said.

'We take all the fittings off the cupboards,' he said. 'As for the wood, I know a firm in Barking who make chipboard. Get them to come and collect it.'

'That will take us ages, Jack, getting all the fittings off.' She folded her arms, adamant. 'We get a skip and throw it all in. The lot. Heave ho, and out. Don't argue with me.'

He took a deep breath. This was it. See how it would go.

'No.'

'Excuse me, Jack. You seem to be forgetting that I am the client here. I am paying you, and you do what I ask.'

He'd been waiting for that. Her ultimate threat.

'OK,' he said. 'Do what you want. But I'm out. I'll give you your money back. And you can get another builder.'

He had no idea whether she would call his bluff. But he had a hold on her. Once off the job, he could go to the police and say how the kitchen had got smashed up. Not that he would, but she couldn't be sure.

'Your decision,' he said.

Lily had returned with two brooms, rubbish bags, rubber gloves and a pan and brush. She stood with the two brooms, like crutches, awaiting orders. Jack signalled her to hold back.

Judy was silent a while, evidently weighing up her options.

'Come outside,' she said.

Not wanting Lily to hear, she led him out into the garden, and onto the lawn. She stopped ten yards from the house, and turned on him.

'You're going to walk out on me?' she said, hands on hips. A challenge.

'If you get a skip. Yes, I'll go.'

She strode about. 'This is nonsense. I might consider it some other time, but we are in a hurry, Jack. There's a wedding on Saturday. We have no time for this green crap.'

He shrugged. 'It's your job. Do what you want. But it won't be with me.'

Her fist was pressed to her mouth. She didn't want him walking off. And he couldn't afford to go. If she fired him, she knew she had no control over him. He had realised last night on the Flats, taking all in all, they were equals in this.

'Make yourself clear,' she said. 'All this extra work you are suggesting. Tell me exactly what.'

'We take the fittings off the cupboards, get the wood taken away by the Barking firm. It will be made into chipboard, giving it a life.' He listed on his fingers. 'For internal doors, flooring, furniture, kitchen cupboards even.'

'Cheap stuff. Inferior quality.'

'Not top quality, sure. That's out of the question, with the wood smashed up. But as chipboard, it won't end up in land-fill. Internal doors can last fifty, a hundred years.'

'And what about the china? Do we stick it back together with spit?'

He had no solution for the china that had broken in the cupboards and fallen from shelves.

'It won't rot in landfill, it's like stone,' was the best he could say. 'It's the wood I want to salvage. Make the best of it.'

'You speak as if you are in charge. As if it is your job.'

'If you want a builder detective, you have to give me some control. We need this to take a little longer. That gives me more time to talk to people, to get to know everyone. Invest-igate who killed your father.'

He realised Judy had been panicking, seeing the destruc-tion she had caused, and wanting it cleared away as soon as possible. With the looming wedding her responsibility, everything had to be right on the day. But she was losing the thread in her need to be in charge. The reason why she had done the demolition in the first place.

'Damn you, Jack. I wish I had never taken you on.'

Ditto, he could have said for his part. With Nova on their case. But he needed to placate Judy. Forget Nova.

Tall order.

'Do it my way,' he said, 'and I will make sure the kitchen is fully repaired before Saturday. If I have work night and day.'

It was an olive branch. He had worked with people like her before. Those who gave orders, and would not be coun-termanded. Even if wrong. But here, he had more power. She didn't want him to leave, not with what he knew, and with her brother banged up in Pentonville, and Jack here to investigate.

She was in a bind, feeling guilty about the destruction and wanting it cleared out of her sight. The kitchen to be clean, tidy, repaired, in kitchen-shape, normal. But her original motive had been to give him work so he could probe.

'A little slower on the work,' he added, 'and I'll get to know everyone better. And find your killer.'

Easy to say, of course, but finishing the work too quickly and he'd be less likely to.

Judy turned away.

'I can't think. I can't think.' Clutching her head, as if in agony.

She walked to the back of the garden, a battle going on inside her, and went into the shed. To do what, he wondered. Hide away? Fire him? Jack looked back to the house. Lily was sitting on a stool, stock still, like a garden gnome.

Judy came out of the shed, holding two pairs of rough leather working gloves.

She marched up to him.

'We'll do it your way.'

Chapter 12

The row over with Judy, Jack organised the work, hoping she wouldn't bear a grudge for too long. He'd have to live with it. Get on with the work. Lily was set to sweeping up, not vacuuming as there were too many splinters and woodchips that would foul the machine. Any large wood in her way was to be taken out to the patio. Once she'd done that, she should clear the worktops.

Judy had already cleared the kitchen island of debris. She was putting on it the intact china: cups, plates, saucers, and bowls, to see how much they had. The same with glasses. She would need to top up the order to the catering firm, as one half of the china they were going to supply themselves, but she knew they no longer had enough, with the breakages.

She had been more than thorough.

Jack worked on the wall cupboards. It was mostly those that had been attacked, plus the shelves. The china within the cupboards and on the shelves had been collateral damage. Cupboards under the worktops had avoided the hammer. The kitchen island had suffered no damage.

There were twelve wall cupboards, all wrecked to a greater or lesser extent. They'd all have to go. Jack began with their doors, taking off the hinges and the handles, one by one. A door, once freed, he put out on the patio. When he had removed all the doors, he could then take down the cupboards.

Though first, they had to be emptied. Some had cans, another pasta, flour and pulses, another herbs and spices. Another had china and jugs, some broken.

Replacement cupboards and shelves were due today, but wouldn't be put up till tomorrow, once the old, damaged ones had all been taken down. He had delayed the process with his refusal to dump the lot in a skip.

Let's see how that played out.

His drill, with a screwdriver bit, made short work of the screws in the hinges. All brass, as were the handles. Somewhat boring, going from cupboard to cupboard, unscrewing the handles and hinges, and putting the door outside. And on to the next. Jack took a break after an hour or so with all the doors off, free of hinges and handles, and stacked on the patio.

He phoned the chipboard firm in Barking. At first they thought he was trying to sell them the broken cupboards. But he assured them, no, he just wanted them to go to a good home. Good solid oak, free for the taking. All the hinges and handles had been removed, he told them. That satisfied them, and they said they would send a van tomorrow afternoon.

Lily was removing items from the cupboards. She was a good worker, anything she was unsure of, she came to him. She put items from the cupboards into large plastic bags, all to go out on the patio for the time being. The food items were kept well away from the salvaged wood and the bags of broken china. It was useful working with her, getting to know her. He couldn't do formal interviews, as only Judy knew he was an investigator. So he had to chat, and throw in the odd question.

Mid morning, the kitchen was tidy enough for a snack break. Lily had made them tea and toast with marmalade. They sat at the island, Jack, Judy and Lily. The intact china at the end. The floor had been swept; it needed a wash but there was no point doing that until the new cupboards had been put in. All three of them had white chippings in their hair, as if they'd been aged ten years.

Things were going at a satisfying pace. Judy had become less fraught as she could see the direction of travel.

'Whoever did this should hang,' said Lily, taking a bite of toast. 'Such lovely cupboards. They have only been up a year. Why do people want to destroy things?'

Neither he or Judy had a reply.

'Mindless vandalism.'

Jack could agree with that. They were first class cupboards. Top of the range, all brass fittings, good oak, well constructed.

'The marquee is coming tomorrow,' said Judy, eager to change the subject of damage. 'I hope the workers can get it out into the garden, with all the stuff on the patio.'

'We'll make room for them,' he said. 'And the wood is being collected by the chipboard firm tomorrow.'

'The sooner this is all straight,' said Lily, 'the happier I shall be. I hate seeing those broken cupboards.'

Not wanting to hear more chat about broken cupboards, Jack seized the opportunity.

'How long have you been working here, Lily?'

'A long time,' she said. 'Before I dyed my hair.' She grinned; she had good teeth, always proof someone wasn't short of money. 'More than twenty years.'

'You must have been a teenager when you started,' he said.

She punched him lightly on the arm. 'Get away with you. My husband had left me. Good riddance to bad rubbish. He never gave me a penny. I had two kids at secondary school. And I had to get work. So I got cleaning work. Put a card in all the houses down these roads. I knew they had money, houses this size. And Mr Ffrench was one of those who took me on. His wife, your mother,' she said to Judy, 'was already ill. So I did the housework, cooked too. Dropped a couple of other jobs as there was plenty here.' She stopped the history. 'These days, I just do a couple of hours a day. I don't need to do more.'

'Do you live nearby?' he said.

'Council flats up the road. Though I've bought mine.'

'That wouldn't be cheap,' said Jack. 'I'm surprised a cleaner could afford it.'

'Housekeeper,' she said, correcting him and looking a little uncomfortable. 'I had a legacy. My father died and left me enough.'

Jack had heard another, more believable, tale on how she had bought her council house. Or rather who had bought it for her.

'Lucky you,' he said.

'And now I must be going,' she said. 'Things to do today.'

'Thank you for helping out,' said Judy. 'Well over your hours.'

'I couldn't leave the kitchen in such a mess. I hope they catch the man who did it.'

She had settled on a man, maybe because of her husband, he thought. Young, old, black, white; who might she pick out in a parade?

Maggie came running in, yelling, 'Look at this!' shaking her phone in the air.

She had their attention, just as there was a ring on the front doorbell.

'I'll get it,' said Lily who was already on the way out.

'See this, see this!' exclaimed Maggie. She was wide eyed, disturbed, frightened, wearing jeans and T-shirt, her hair wet. 'I turned my phone on. I'd been in the bath, haven't had time to dry my hair. And this message came.'

Jack and Judy looked at the phone. There was an email message in capitals:

SECOND WARNING. YOU DIE IF YOU MARRY HIM.

Lily came to the kitchen door.

'It's the cupboards, just arrived,' she said.

'Put them in the hallway,' said Judy. 'No, wait. I'd best check them.' She followed Lily out.

Jack sat Maggie down and poured her a cup of tea.

'That is one nasty message,' he said. 'Have you had them before?'

'No. What shall I do, Jack?'

'Go to the police. Might be just hot air, but it is as well to alert them.'

She looked at him, appealing. 'Will you come with me?'

That was a surprise, but a chance to talk to her on the way.

'Finish your tea. I'll check with Judy.'

He went out into the hall. Judy was standing by the stack of flat cardboard packs that the cupboards had come in. He looked them over: the wood, hinges, handles, brackets, screws and instructions would all be in the box. Not a surprise. Easy enough to assemble. In addition, there were six long packs, obviously the shelves.

Judy was going through the delivery note with the driver. Lily had gone.

'Maggie wants me to go to the police station with her,' he said.

Judy looked up quizzically.

'With that threatening message,' he said. 'Be a good chance to chat with her on the way.'

'Go then,' said Judy. He'd been expecting an argument, but maybe she was argued out. And the work had begun well, the cupboards had come. Besides which, he wasn't just a builder. Plenty of work in the kitchen maybe, but he was no wiser on who murdered Judy's father.

'Cupboards all here,' Judy said to the delivery man. 'I just need to check on the shelving...'

Jack left her and went back into the kitchen.

'Let's go,' he said to Maggie.

Chapter 13

Judy was on the phone to Pentonville as they left for the police station, arranging a visit to Cliff. Which would be for him and her. Jack would need an excuse to explain his absence from work. A funeral, that usually worked. Grandmother again. He'd been to three of those.

Maggie wore a woolly hat as her hair was damp. Though hardly necessary, he figured, in this warm weather. A ten minute walk, at most.

The sun was shining and he was pleased to be out of the house. The stress of the argument with Judy still festered. It had been no small thing threatening to walk off of a job and give one thousand pounds back. In the end, she'd agreed to go his way, but not before pushing him to the brink.

All over not much more than a few hours' work. That's how long it had taken to get the fittings off. Judy was for throwing them all in a skip. And was fighting all the way. If he hadn't had a hold on her, knowing she'd smashed the cupboards, and his undercover work, he'd have caved. He needed the money, and the boss was the boss.

Except when she wasn't quite.

That email message. Second warning, it said. What was the first? A death threat if she married. Heavy stuff. But it didn't quite make sense.

One thing at a time. The job was going OK, so far, and that seemed to have mellowed Judy. The kitchen was clean, all the doors were off the damaged cupboards, with a pyramid of fittings one end of the island. He'd have those. Mia could sell them on her stall at the festival, Saturday. Day of the wedding too.

He was only paid till then. Well paid, but Judy wanted the case cleared up. A lady in a hurry and maybe asking too much of him. The investigation was barely in the foothills. He hadn't met Uncle Alec, nor been to see Cliff, though that was being set up. He had had only brief chats with Mo and Tom.

But that message. Did it connect to the murder? Or the impending marriage? Or both? Was it just a frightener?

This was always the low point in a case. When it was all questions and no answers.

'Thank you so much for coming with me,' said Maggie. 'I didn't want to phone Mo about the threatening message. He would only want to come straight over. And what could he do anyway?'

'Don't say that to him.'

She smiled. 'I won't.'

'Why didn't you want to go with Judy?'

She threw up her hands. 'Oh, she just takes over everything.'

'She has that habit,' he said, knowing full well. But time was short; he needed to dig, while he had her on her own. 'Any idea who could have sent the message?'

They were going the back way, down Osborne Road, few people walked on these well-heeled streets. It was an easy pace which pacified Maggie, and suited him, cutting through Richmond Road to the Romford Road, no rush, getting her talking. Pointless driving with the hassle of parking. And much easier to talk as they walked.

'Mo's father,' she said. 'I bet it was him. He's not coming to the wedding. Marrying a white girl. Oh shock, horror. Haram!' She translated for Jack. 'It means forbidden. Of all Mo's family, just his brother is coming; his sister was going to come but her husband forbade her. What a doormat!'

'What does Mo feel about them not coming?'

'He shrugs it off, but I know he cares. Not that he gets on with his father. One of the many things we have in common. Bullying fathers.' She put a hand on Jack's arm and said in a hushed voice. 'That message. They could be threatening an honour killing.'

'It said second warning. What was the first?'

She thought for a while, then said, 'Smashing up the kitchen. That must be it. They did it.'

'You think so?'

Knowing they hadn't, he almost wanted to tell her why.

'It fits,' she insisted. 'Wrecking the kitchen shows they mean business, and they can get in any time they want.' She stopped walking at a thought, holding him back by the arm. 'We must change the locks!'

'OK.' He would discuss it with Judy, though knowing it was a waste of money. But it made sense as he and she were sticking to the intruder tale. And Maggie would feel better for it. There were two locks on the front door, expensive ones. He'd keep the old locks. A bonus. He was always needing locks on one job or another.

Maggie had persuaded herself it was Mo's family. Another reading of the bones, and it almost held. A domineering father, Mo disgracing the family, marrying a non-Muslim white girl. It could be made to fit. He knew wrecking the kitchen had nothing to do with the message, but it was easy to see how she could connect the two.

'How did you and Mo meet?' he said, to get off the subject.

'We met at a festival in Essex. Judy had got me a gig there, an event she was organising. She gets me at least half my gigs. Anyway, I'd done my spot, and had gone along to a guitar workshop. I play but I'm still awkward and not confident. Mo was there with his guitar, I didn't know him. But he invited me for a coffee afterwards and we just got on.'

'So he's musical too.'

'Not bad. A good amateur. Mo wouldn't mind me saying that. He admits it. But the thing is,' she went on, 'we might not have met at all. He was supposed to be at the festival with his fiancée, a Muslim girl that the family had fixed him up with. She'd said she would go, then she had pulled out, said there'd be drugs and drinking. Well, there was some, but it wasn't exactly a drugs den, the odd spliff, a beer tent. Anyway, we got together, and he broke off the engagement.

What a hullabaloo that was! His father stopped talking to him, the ex fiancée's brothers beat him up. But that was four months ago. Water under the bridge, you'd think.'

'And your father, how did he take it?'

She threw her arms up. 'Just as bad. Or even worse. Like in *Fairytale of New York*. You know, by the Pogues.' She sang, '*You're a slut, you're a whore, get out of my house! You're no daughter of mine.*'

The words weren't right, he knew, she was improvising. Mo was right though, she had a good voice. He could almost enjoy being insulted by her. In song at least.

Maggie smiled wanly. 'You have to laugh, it's so stupid in this day and age. Like a Victorian novel. On Mo's part, I accept breaking off an engagement is not a good look, but it was not like he was sleeping with her. Good Muslim girl, she wouldn't have that. No way. But I'm the slut of the tale, four months gone now. Dad never knew, not that he could think any worse of me. Your kids will be mongrels!' She paused, thinking back. 'Dad actually said that. Those words. He wouldn't let Mo in the house. I moved in with him. Came back only after Dad's death.'

'He didn't cut you out of the will?'

'That was such a close thing.' She squeezed two fingers almost together. 'A hair's breadth. Dad was talking to his solicitor. I was certain for the chop. And Tom for being gay, Cliff for being an artist, though you'd hardly think that was deviant, and Judy for calling him out. She'd rage at him.'

He was glad to get a refresher on the draft will, as he had been barely paying attention last night. His mind on other things.

The new will in the offing gave all the siblings a reason to kill their father. If it had gone through, they'd all be cut out of any inheritance. As it was they'd all done very well.

'I've written a song about it,' she said. 'Not quite right. Needs some rewriting. Sort of modelled on *Fairytale of New York*. Though it's between a woman and her father-in-law with no shmaltzy Christmas making up at the end. Me and

Mo made a recording of it. Just in our room. He's not a bad singer, can hold a tune, but it needs someone stronger for the father-in-law. He knows that. Anyway, where was I?'

She recollected. 'The will that didn't happen. Oh yes. Dad died in the nick of time. Murdered, let's call it what it was. The new will didn't get signed, and the old one gave a decent slice to a slut, a queer, an artist and an uppity woman. Poetic justice you might say. Dad must be turning in his grave. Hard cheese, old man. Cliff did us a favour, but I so hope it wasn't him. But then he confessed. I am fond of Cliff, we are creatives. Me a singer songwriter, him an artist, we are bonded. Prison must be killing him. He is so sensitive.'

Her eyes welled.

'Awful places,' said Jack. 'They crush you.'

'Have you been inside?'

'A few weeks, too long, for something I didn't do. Got off, thank God.'

'I must go and see him. Once the wedding is over, and we've got to the bottom of this message business. It has me by the throat. I am absolutely sure Mo's family are behind it. Smashing up the kitchen, following up with the threat to kill me. Why can't they just leave us alone?'

'No one hates like families,' he said.

'Or loves.'

They were at the police station. It had been an informative walk. She was hyper and talkative, like the truth drug, telling him heaps about herself and Mo, more than she might have done had it been just a walk without the email to get her going. He had been supportive, her confidant. How would she react to finding out he was a private detective? Quizzing her for his own motives.

Chapter 14

The desk officer, once he'd been shown the email and told who were the investigating officers, phoned through on the internal network.

In a few minutes, Nova came for them. Dressed as usual in her navy suit trousers, never a skirt. Better to run in, she'd told him, and not showing knickers in a fight. Practical and dignified, that was Nova, her blonde hair tied back in a pony-tail. Just the person to pacify Maggie, but not him. He was agitated in her presence, glad he wasn't here alone.

Who was supporting whom?

Nova took them behind the front desk, further into the station, and into a small room off the main corridor. A boring room, nothing on the yellow walls, frosted glass on the window, a faint hum of traffic coming through. The only furniture was a table and three plastic chairs.

Nova got the picture almost at once, being familiar with the case. Maggie did all the talking, insisting it must be Mo's family. They had smashed the kitchen, that was the warning referred to, and now a death threat.

'These are often empty threats,' said Nova, indicating the message on the phone.

'You don't know Mo's family,' insisted Maggie.

'True,' she allowed. 'We'll send someone round. If it is them and they realise we suspect them, they'll surely stop. Let me have their contact details.'

From her phone, Maggie gave the address and phone number of Mo's parents. 'Only been there once. Down in Plaistow, near the Greenway. I couldn't get out fast enough. His father deliberately speaking Urdu so I wouldn't understand. But I knew all right, with the odd word of English coming through and his father looking at me like I'd just crawled out of the gutter.'

Nova rose.

'I'll action a visit. And let me have your phone.' Maggie hesitated. 'Just for a few minutes. We might get something from the metadata.'

Maggie handed it over. Nova left them, saying she wouldn't be long.

Jack had barely said a word. It was mostly Maggie speaking with Nova interjecting. He wondered how Nova was fitting the two events. Yesterday she was sure that he and Judy had smashed up the kitchen. Now with the message, he hoped she had shifted somewhat, not knowing whether the two events were connected or not. She couldn't discount that they were.

Someone had done him and Judy a favour.

Maggie shivered. 'These rooms are dreadful. Make you feel guilty just being in them.'

'They are meant to be uncomfortable,' he said. 'No distractions.'

'I wonder whether Cliff was in here. This very one. Maybe writing his confession on this table.'

A police constable came in with two coffees and a pack of biscuits.

'Compliments of the house,' he said with a grin, placing them on the table.

They thanked him and he left.

'It's an attempt to make us feel comfortable,' he said.

'Doesn't work,' she said. 'I can't help thinking of Cliff being in here.'

They drank the coffee and nibbled the biscuits. Something to do, in this mind-numbing room.

'How do you get on with Tom?' he said.

'Mostly OK. He played the bongos on my last album. That makes it sound like I've made hundreds, like Madonna or someone. Three actually. Tom did an English degree at

Oxford, and now writes those stupid jingles. But he's OK; anyone Dad hated is OK. Nancy boy, Dad would call him, to his face too. Tom would make a joke of it, which infuriated Dad. He made a sort of jingle of it. How did it go? It is so stupid. Dad threw a jug at him. It missed and smashed.' She recited:

> 'Nancy beat Sycophancy on the bum
> It was her fancy, was it for Nancy
> when feeling romancy with a tot of rum

An Oxford degree reduced to doggerel! All those college fees. Can you credit?'

Jack laughed. With his lack of formal education he liked hearing tales of educated halfwits.

Nova returned. She didn't sit down.

'Mo's parents are getting a visit,' she said. 'Just in case. If they or one of the extended family sent the message, that should discourage them.' She handed back the phone. 'One of our IT experts is checking the metadata on the phone. She says it's unlikely they'll track it back, but she'll have a go. Just a generic email address, anyone can get. Trolls get them by the score. But if you get any more such messages, let me know at once.'

That was hardly confidence boosting, thought Jack.

'We need to change the front door locks,' said Maggie. 'Wouldn't you say?'

Nova sucked her bottom lip, weighing this up. He knew what he would say to a client: your money, you spend it how you like. Though somewhat more politely.

'Not a bad idea,' said Nova. 'To be on the safe side.'

Two hundred quid down the drain.

Chapter 15

They walked more swiftly back. Maggie was feeling better after Nova had taken her seriously. Mo's parents were getting a visit from the cops, and a tech expert was examining the metadata of the message.

Arriving back, Maggie opened the front door.

'You go in,' Jack said. 'I want to look at the locks.'

'Thank you so much for coming, Jack. I know it's not your job, but I needed it.' She gave him a peck on the cheek, 'Above and beyond the call of duty. I'll make us some toast.'

She went in.

At least, she was happier, even if he felt guilty about his subterfuge.

Jack had a close look at the two locks on the front door. Although perfectly good locks, it was more than likely they'd had to go. Maggie was insisting Mo's father, or at least one of the family, had smashed the kitchen as a warning to her. So must have a key as there was no sign of a break in. He and Judy were in no position to argue. In fact, supporting her was in their interest.

When it came to the locks, he might as well replace like for like. A much simpler job, take the old locks out and put the new ones in, with no drilling or chiselling needed.

He jotted down the lock details, and hoped the locksmith would have them in stock.

And being outside, there was no time like the present, he phoned the police station, asking for Nova. Sure, he'd seen her fifteen minutes ago, but he had been with Maggie, so couldn't say what he wanted.

She answered, saying, 'So soon, Jack.'

'I couldn't talk before,' he said. 'It's about the murder of Richard Ffrench. I hear there is a draft will. Have you got it?'

'We most certainly have. Fascinating reading.'

'Can you let me have it?'

'Not you. No.'

'You have to disclose evidence to the defendant.'

'That's Cliff Ffrench and his lawyer. Not you.'

'Could you let Judy Ffrench have it?'

'You are asking a lot, Jack.'

He was thinking, you certainly owe me, Nova. Much more than a draft will.

'Don't ask, don't get,' he said. A childhood mantra.

'I'll ask Fayyad, but don't build your hopes up.'

'Thanks for having a go.'

They rang off. It was hard talking to her, but easier on the phone than face to face. He'd barely said a word at the cop shop. Not that he'd needed to, Maggie being so hyper.

He thought about the draft will. If he couldn't see it, and they wouldn't let Judy see it either, then their other option was through Cliff, who hopefully they'd be seeing tomorrow. It could well be why Richard Ffrench was murdered. To stop it being actioned. Essential that he see it.

Call ended, Jack went into the house and down the hallway to the kitchen.

Judy and Maggie were there, with an elderly man who instantly confronted Jack.

'Are you the builder?' he demanded.

His white hair was thin on top, surrounding a shiny scalp. He wore a brown suit, with a light blue shirt and brown tie to match the suit. Shiny black leather shoes. Jack always looked at shoes. They tell you so much about the wearer. These said conventional, old fashioned, a stickler for tidiness.

'I'm the builder, yes,' he said.

'So what are you doing taking her to the police station?' He pointed out Maggie.

Jack was certainly getting it in the neck today.

'I asked him to,' said Maggie. She was making toast. 'How many slices, Jack?'

'A couple, thanks.'

'He is your builder,' insisted the man, pointing him out as if the others might not have noticed him. 'And you have a wrecked kitchen. He should have been here. Working. Why didn't you take her to the police station, Judy?'

Judy was on a stool at the island, doing some paperwork. She didn't look up.

'I was waiting for the cupboards, Uncle Alec.'

She wasn't. They had already come. But neither he or Maggie were going to correct her.

'He should have waited for the cupboards, not you, while you accompanied your sister to the police station.'

'I am here,' said Maggie, waving a buttery knife. 'See, see, here. Look!'

So this was the mythical Uncle Alec. He couldn't imagine having a natter with him over coffee and cake. Builders should have no time for idle chats.

'I had calls to make,' said Judy. 'I had to be here. There's a wedding on Saturday, unless you've forgotten.'

'A rush job,' he harrumphed.

'The locks need changing, Judy,' said Maggie, ignoring him. 'Whoever got in to smash up the kitchen, could well come again.'

Judy looked to Jack, both knowing they didn't need changing at all.

'The police woman said so,' said Maggie.

She had hardly, thought Jack. Nova had somewhat mildly gone along with Maggie.

'Isn't that so, Jack?'

'Yes, she did.'

Not really a lie, or far less than the tale that necessitated the changing of locks in Maggie's eyes.

'It needs doing right away. Please.'

'My dear girl...' began Uncle Alec.

'I am in danger!'

'Get the locks,' said Judy to Jack.

'There is a kitchen to be repaired!' yelled Uncle Alec to the room.

'What about my life!' yelled Maggie back at him.

'They're going to cost well over 200 quid,' said Jack. 'With extra keys, two fifty plus I'd say.'

He was trying to intimate that he didn't want to lay out all that cash.

Judy caught on.

'Come on,' she said. 'My car. I'll pay. Let's go get them.'

She headed for the door, Jack in her wake.

'Take some toast, Jack!'

He grabbed a couple of slices, then followed Judy, who always seemed to be rushing.

'This is a mad house!' Uncle Alec was yelling, as they left, fuming to Maggie.

Whatever else he said was lost to Jack as he headed after Judy. Though he could well imagine. Not much fun for Maggie being left with an angry old man. But then she wanted locks.

Chapter 16

He ate the toast while Judy drove to the locksmith in Manor Park. A five minute drive.

'I'm spending money like water,' said Judy. 'Though we could hardly deny her new locks. As we have to insist on an intruder doing the damage. Don't you think?'

'Yes.' Having started lying, he had no course but keep up the tale, for both their sakes. He added, 'The threatening message makes DS Taylor less certain it was me and you did it.'

'Then maybe it's worth two fifty quid.'

The journey was straight down the road, there was little traffic, the odd car as they passed the double fronted Victorian houses. Good for work, well off clients, noting where he'd worked over the years. Like a journey through time.

'I have fixed up our prison visit,' she said. 'Tomorrow at three. Get your excuse ready.'

'Grandma's funeral. I'll get in early and slave away all morning.' Though just Maggie would be at home, not counting Judy, with Tom and Mo at work, and Lily long gone. He was getting into the habit of lying. To the cops, to everyone in the house. It was bound to come back and bite him.

That garden wall was his. A few years back. Useful work, unlike his futile work at the moment. What with destroyed cupboards and now locks that didn't need renewing. It was wearying.

'What did you make of Uncle Alec?' she said.

'Quite a powder keg,' he said. 'He didn't like me going off with Maggie to the cop shop, or with you. He has a short fuse. I'd hate to be one of his workers.'

79

'You should have heard him with Dad. The two of them yelling so all the street could listen in. As teenagers, we just kept out of their way. Fortunately, Dad was mostly out working, but when the two got together here... That last Christmas! I can't even remember what they were arguing about. They'd both drunk too much. Peanut butter, it was about peanut butter. Who had invented it. It was potty, loony. Maggie and Mo hadn't come, and I'd been in two minds, but thought I'd best support Tom and Cliff. Those two old fogies have been arguing for the best part of fifty years. Except,' she paused for a few seconds, turning a thought over, then pulling up at the side of the road.

'The big birthday do, Dad's 70th.'

'The night he was murdered.'

'Dad was getting drunk, but not Uncle Alec, he was cuddling a bottle of some foul herbal thing, I took a sniff, non alcoholic. Dad kept taunting Uncle Alec, and all he would say back was, "There he goes again". We'd all been tossing up whether to come to his do. All pull out in solidarity, show him what we thought of him. The four of us making some excuse, but then Dad promised a big surprise.' She stopped as a thought hit her. 'He allowed Mo to come. That was odd, don't you think?'

'From all I have heard, yes.'

'But he never got round to his big surprise. Got too drunk, his stomach playing up, and he went to bed. And then there was a very big surprise, but that had to wait till morning when Lily found him.'

'But what do you think his surprise was?'

'The new will, we all think. I think he was going to read it to us, shell-shock us, and then, in front of us all, very dramatically, sign it.'

'What do you think was in it?'

'Bad news for most of us for sure. But Uncle Alec knew. I am sure he kept sober on purpose. He had wind something was on, and it was going to be in his favour.'

'Your father had the lion's share of the shares. Uncle Alec only had a fraction.'

'Dad had put more money in at the beginning, so was able to give Uncle Alec the squeeze. Some sharp dealing there, I don't really know what. I think really that's what the arguments were about over the years. Never mind the subject.'

'Your dad was the boss.'

'Undoubtedly, but Uncle Alec couldn't be sacked. He had 10% of the shares. A junior partner, somehow that got written into their initial agreement. He earned a good salary as manager though; Dad needed someone as cut-throat as he was.'

'I pity the staff.'

'Not a happy place to work under those two. Easier though as the business got bigger. They couldn't be everywhere.'

You got your share, he thought. Nice people employing oppressive managers, so they can keep their hands clean.

She started driving again. Thoughts on Uncle Alec delivered. Had to be a suspect, amongst the many. Staying sober at the do.

'I phoned DS Taylor,' he said, 'asking her whether they had a copy of the draft will,' he said. 'They do. I asked her if we can have it. She tells me, she'll ask her boss if they can send us a copy, but she's not hopeful he'll give permission.'

'That doesn't surprise me.'

'She told me it was fascinating.'

'Presumably meaning Dad was going to give the whole shebang to a cats' home.'

'Do you think that was likely?'

'It would be the sort of mean trick he'd pull. Sort of saying to us all, start being nice to me and I might rewrite it. And damn the cats.'

She halted at Romford Road, and once it was clear, turned onto it, parking a short way up, in front of the locksmith's.

Once in the shop, Jack knew what he wanted. The same locks as on the door now. It was painful to think about spending two fifty getting to the same place. A waste, but it wasn't his two fifty. And he'd collar the old locks.

He searched through the various locks on display. They were in luck, the shop had both the ones on the door. Each had three keys.

'How many keys do you need? he asked.

Judy enumerated on her fingers; 'Me, Maggie, Mo, Tom, Lily, Uncle Alec, don't know why for him, tradition, and best have a set for Cliff. And a spare set. That's eight. Let's make it ten.'

It took quarter of an hour to get the extra keys cut. Jack looked at the tools in the shop, while Judy made phone calls. From what he could hear of her side, an event somewhere in two weeks. Busy lady. How could she remember it all?

They were called when the cutting was complete. Judy paid up, and they left.

Chapter 17

As soon as they were back at the house, Jack took out a few tools from his van and set about renewing the two locks on the front door. Removing the old ones, and putting in the new, was as easy as he had expected it to be. The holes already cut when the old locks had been put in; it just needed a little chiselling to fit the new. The new locks in, he tried the keys. A little stiff, he gave the locks some grease. And had both working well. Satisfying, if totally bonkers. He put the old locks in the hallway for the time being. His bonus. Now he needed to gather up the old keys.

He went into the kitchen. Judy was there on her own, on the phone. From what she was saying he gathered it was about the marquee. Some hassle, she was quite sharp, reminding the contractor about a festival in Hampshire in a few weeks.

She came off the phone.

'They wanted to bring the marquee on Friday,' she said. 'I made it clear, I am not having that. Too chancy, with the wedding on Saturday. I told them it has to be tomorrow. And now it is.'

'The new locks are in,' he said. He had all the keys. 'Can I have your keys for the old locks?'

'What will you do with them?'

She sorted out the two old keys from her bunch, and he gave her the two new.

'I always need locks,' he said, wondering whether she might claim them. 'But they are yours if you want them.'

'Take them,' she said. 'Get them out of my sight.'

'I'll put them in the van. Where's Uncle Alec and Maggie?'

'He's watching TV. He thinks he can turn up any time he likes, and then harangue us like his shop staff. Dad gave him keys to the house. Heaven knows why, considering their shouting matches. Maggie is in her room working on a song.'

'Is that tea fresh?' he said, indicating the teapot.

'Pretty fresh.'

He took a mug, added milk, and poured out the tea. He put the mug on a small tray with a plate of biscuits, with two new keys.

'I'll take these into Uncle Alec, get his old keys and see if I can get him talking.'

'The cupboards, Jack. Please.' She indicated the door-less, broken ones on the walls. 'Time is passing. Please.'

She was certainly anxious, but not having a go at him. Pleading for him to get on with it. Which was all to the good, as rows soured everything, and lived with you all day.

'They will all be off the walls today,' he said. 'I promise you. If I have to stay till midnight. And the new ones go up tomorrow.'

'Don't forget our visit to Cliff tomorrow afternoon.'

'I've allowed for that. They'll be up tomorrow. When we get back from Pentonville, I'll get straight down to it. Don't worry, you'll have your cupboards, bright spanking new, to impress all the neighbours.'

Jack doubted they'd be impressed even as he said it, being no different from the ones there yesterday morning. Ditto the locks. He felt as if he was walking on the spot, so much effort to catch up with himself.

He picked up the tray.

'Three teaspoons of sugar in the tea,' she said. 'Uncle Alec has a very sweet tooth.'

Jack sugared the tea.

'And think cupboards, cupboards, and more cupboards.'

'I get the message, ma'am. Loud and clear.' He mock saluted.

It was obvious why she wanted them done and the old out the way pronto. Her guilt. She yearned to have the new ones

84

in, the old far, far away, so she could forget about her hammering frenzy.

Jack went into the TV room. Uncle Alec was on the sofa watching an episode of *Flog It*, one of those shows where contestants try to buy cheap from antique shops and make money when the items are auctioned. He'd never watched it intentionally, but caught it every so often in clients' houses. It seemed to have been running forever.

'Anything but building work,' said Uncle Alec, seeing him with the tray. 'Now you're the teas maid.'

He considered doing an about turn, and taking the tray back to the kitchen. But that would get him nowhere. Uncle Alec was an old man, stewed in his rudeness.

'The new front door locks are in,' he said, not rising to the slight. 'Here's your new keys. Can I have your old ones?'

Uncle Alec searched through his pockets, and came up with his keys, handing over the old for the new. The TV programme burbled on in the background. A woman was trying to buy an old pocket watch in an antique shop and was haggling over the price.

'I can't eat those biscuits,' said Uncle Alec. 'My diabetes. Biscuits are out.'

So is heavily sugared tea. Though Jack could hardly criticise considering his own carelessness on diet matters.

'I've got it too,' he said. 'Type two.'

'You!' said Uncle Alec in surprise. 'You are way too young.'

'Too much junk food.'

'Boozing?'

'I'm off booze.' Most of the time, he could have added. 'Fry ups are my downfall.'

'I'm off booze too,' said Uncle Alec. 'That's why I am so miserable. This house doesn't help. Don't know why I come, they don't listen to me. You're working in the kitchen, well some of the time you are, when you are not off to the cop shop, buying locks and bringing tea round. Tell me, what is going on in this loony bin?'

Jack wanted to be asking the questions, but had to answer some too or Uncle Alec would usher him out. The same woman was haggling over an early edition of *Wuthering Heights*. And wasn't going to get it.

'An intruder came in,' he began, 'and smashed the cupboards in the kitchen,' relating the old fable, almost getting to believe it himself, having said it so often. 'Maggie got a threatening message and says it has come from Mo's family. She thinks, they were the ones who smashed the kitchen, to show her they can get in any time, and will kill her if she marries Mo. Which is why I changed the locks.' It was all tumbling out of him and sounding far fetched. 'Her brother, Cliff, has confessed to the murder of Mr Ffrench but Judy thinks he's innocent. Maggie is not sure.'

One of those should get Uncle Alec talking, surely.

'Innocent as Hitler,' said Uncle Alec. 'The boy confessed. Why should he do that if he's not guilty? And I'll tell you why he did it. Dickie Ffrench was going to sign the new will in front of them all, at his birthday do, cutting those spoilt brats back to the bone. And it would have served them right.'

Jack wondered why it would serve them right, but figured he'd just get a moan about ingratitude. Or some such. Though Uncle Alec still dropped into the house of the spoilt brats whenever he felt like it.

'We worked for it, me and Dickie,' went on Uncle Alec, 'slaved away, all the hours God sends, built up the business, deal on deal over nearly fifty years. What have they done? Tell me, Mr Builder.'

'Not a lot,' he agreed. Money goes to money, the way the world worked. 'So Mr Ffrench was going to cut them out?'

'And how. Give them some dregs.'

'Who'd be the winners?' he asked. 'In the new will.'

'Me and Lily were due to take it all in trumps.' He slapped his thigh in anger. 'But that arty farty nobody did him in. Where's the justice?'

That could have been a big discussion point. Who gets rich and how, unearned income and justice, but not with this man.

'Did you see the will, sir?'

He couldn't very well call him Uncle Alec.

'No, but Dickie Ffrench told me in private. Said he'd dreamed of seeing all their dismayed faces when he showed the new will and they saw how little they were getting.'

'How did you know he was telling the truth?'

He shrugged. 'I didn't. Could have been a bag of wind. Just like Dickie Ffrench to have us all on. Not that it matters now. I got no more than I had, and that is that. Too clever by half was Dickie boy. Cheated me from the off. And stole my girl. Long time ago. I was going out with Wendy Harper before the old swindler muscled in. Had the cheek to invite me to their wedding. I had to buy the old chiseller a present. Got his comeuppance though. One of his kids did for him. I tell you, I didn't mourn him long. Almost cheered when the coffin slid down to the furnace.' He stopped for an instant. 'Why am I telling you this? Who are you? Are you really a builder?'

He was looking at Jack suspiciously. 'Not seeing much work done but doing a heap of quizzing. Tell me why, sonny jim.'

'I'm keen to learn how you old guys made it,' he blustered, 'what fires up, you entrepreneurs, so I can have a go myself.'

'The one you needed to learn from is Dickie Ffrench, late of this parish.' He laughed. 'I just got the crumbs from his table. Let me tell you a true fact. In every self made man's rise to fortune, there's one great big dirty deed. Now you know what to do, sonny, get out there, do some work, instead of gassing with me, and screw someone. And mind you lay off the cake and fry ups. And while you are in the kitchen, tell Judy nose-in-the-air I'd like a cheese and tomato sandwich.'

'Thank you so much, sir,' said Jack. 'I've learnt a lot.'

He left, having learnt why he'd never be rich. He hadn't rich parents and lacked the mean gene.

Out in the hallway, he gathered up the two locks, and took them out to his van. Coming back in, he went up the stairs.

Chapter 18

He could hear guitar playing and singing through the door. A pleasant voice, the guitar rhythmic, though he wasn't much of a judge. He couldn't quite make out the words, but then he often couldn't make out the words of songs. Mia had to tell him what they were about. Telling him, for instance that Tom Jones' *Delilah* was about a murderer who has killed the woman he loves. He had thought the man was just desperately in love. That bit was true, but he'd missed the knifing; the real reason for all the weeping and wailing.

Jack waited for a break in the singing, then rapped on the door.

'Come in,' said Maggie.

He opened the door and entered the large master bedroom, wider than it was deep, going the full width of the house, with two large windows. Maggie was in the corner of the room facing the door by one of the windows. She put down her guitar as he came in. A music stand was in front of her, with a sheet of handwritten guitar chords full of crossings out. To one side was a keyboard on a stand. Other bits of gear were nearby: microphones, an amplifier, speakers, a pile of sheet music and assorted electronic bits and pieces that he wasn't sure what they were. Music paraphernalia for recording and playing, most likely.

That section of the room was her domain, the rest was bedroom with a sitting room element, housing a large made bed with a blue and yellow coverlet matching the long curtains on the windows. At the top end of the bed, like a mascot, was Paddington Bear, in duffle coat and floppy hat. He wondered which of the two claimed him. There were two wardrobes, a chest of drawers, a dressing table, a desk with a small TV on it, and chairs here and there, and a sofa. How many sofas did this house have? Four so far, he made it, three more than he had.

Here, Richard Ffrench had been strangled. In this room, but a very different room. He was curious about the changes, but he had the disturbing feeling that the woman with the engaging voice, could be the murderer, with a song to match *Delilah*. '*Forgive me Daddy, I just couldn't take any more!*'

No, no, there were plenty of other suspects, including one in jail who had confessed.

'Sorry to interrupt you, Maggie,' he said, quelling his mean thoughts, 'but I've put the new locks in the front door, and here's your keys. Can I have your old ones?'

'You haven't interrupted me. This song isn't working. The lyrics are not right, flat, the tune isn't catching the emotion. I have to feel it when I'm singing. It needs to soar. I throw more than half of my songs away, and this might be another for the bin.'

She was fishing through her handbag, and came up with a bunch of keys. She took two off their rings and handed them over.

'Let me have Mo's new keys too,' she said. 'I'll get the old ones off him for you.'

'Thanks.' He took the old keys and gave her the new ones for her and Mo, still taking in the room. Big, tidy, but with such a history; he couldn't rid himself of the notion that she might be the murderer. So slight, that pretty elfin cut, so innocent and guilty.

'Yes,' she said. 'This is where it happened.'

'I didn't mean to gawp.'

Not giving away that he'd gone the extra mile, and had her as a prime suspect. But then again, every one of the inhabitants of this house could be the killer, unless it was the man in jail. This, though, was the room where the strangling took place, and here she was singing a song of love. Wouldn't the killer have taken another room?

Unless he was underestimating her cruelty.

'Only natural, Jack, to be curious,' she said. 'Who wouldn't be? I know I would be rubbernecking. But me and Mo, before moving in, we stripped the room bare, getting rid of him. We gave his clothes to charity. His papers are in the loft, heaven knows what for, just his business stuff, as if he were famous. The British Heart Foundation had the bed, the furniture, the curtains and the carpet, and good riddance to it all. The room was left utterly empty. We had it redecorated, floor sanded, new carpet laid, new curtains and all new furniture. Nothing is left of him.'

The space itself, he thought. The walls, the floor, the ceiling, in these confines, it happened.

'Doesn't it feel just a little creepy?' he said, and wondering whether he should be saying so, even as he was speaking. The murdered man was, after all, her father. But Jack was hoping to get an inkling of her guilt or otherwise. So march in, mob handed.

'Not at all. Dad's gone, burnt to ashes. Someone unknown has his bed, now that would be creepy, sleeping in that, but they won't know. We threw away the mattress though, too stained. I'd hate to have slept on that. And old man's stains.' She shuddered. 'I'm not at all sorry he's dead. I can't help it. He was so nasty to Mo.'

A motive there. And the money, never forget the cash. He'd learnt that from his first investigation.

'Your father left you a share of his business,' he said.

'Dad was going to cut us all out. So I hear. Apparently, there was a draft will where all the family would be shafted.' She shrugged. 'Water under the bridge. Dad missed the boat. Oh, that's an extended metaphor. I should write it down.' She trilled, '*Water under the bridge, I missed your boat. Lover, come sail with me.*' She stopped singing, laughing at her effort. 'Doesn't make sense, but I might mess around with it. Could be a chorus. No idea what goes in the verses. I want to have enough songs for another album. I've a few gigs coming up.'

'How will motherhood affect you?'

'That is so scary, Jack. I have been reading about mother-hood. How it takes you over. I don't want to write songs about mum and her beautiful baby. I am going to bottle feed, so much easier. It means when I have a gig, Mo can look after baby. These days, Mo goes with me to gigs, to support me. I'll have to go on my own. I suppose that's what kids do to you. Complicate your life, squeeze your time, what with nappies, baby formula, crying all night, getting ill. But I am not stopping gigging. We are agreed.'

'I'd like to come and see you perform.' That was genuine, not a detective speaking. She was not simply a suspect but a good singer too. 'Where was your last gig?'

'A folk club in Islington.' She snapped her fingers. 'Mo took some video on my phone.' She stretched for her phone and switched it on. 'I have it off when I'm composing. Or it's like the man from Porlock, and you lose your thread after a call.'

Jack wondered about the man from Porlock, something to do with losing your thread, but why Porlock, wherever that was, but he didn't ask as it wasn't pertinent. As this was Forest Gate, and this was the room where it had happened.

'I have so much on this phone,' she said, 'takes ages to load up. Must give it a clear out, too many junk photos. Ah that's it.' She tapped a couple of buttons. 'Oh, no,' suddenly aghast. 'Another one!'

She held out the phone. Jack took it from her. He read:
THIRD WARNING. MARRY MO AND YOU ARE DEAD MEAT.

'I thought that was all done with,' she said, eyes welling.

'From the same sender as before,' he said, looking at the address. 'We must phone Nova...' He corrected himself. 'We must phone DS Taylor.'

'You do it, Jack. I feel sick. They want to kill me. Mo's family. They want to make sure the wedding doesn't happen.'

'Most of these threats aren't real,' he said. 'Just online bravado.' He was going to say, they can be vicious because

91

they are anonymous. But felt that was no comfort. 'I'll phone the police,' he added.

He had Nova's personal number, her work one too. He considered which, and dialled the personal as she might be out and about, while feeling guilty about his former thoughts about Maggie and her part in her father's death.

'Hello, Jack,' said Nova. 'I can't talk long. I'm out on a case.'

He put her on speaker phone, so Maggie could hear.

'Maggie Ffrench has had another threatening email. From the same sender. She's with me now.'

'Put her on.'

Jack gave Maggie the phone.

'I'm sorry, Maggie,' said Nova, 'but we haven't yet visited your fiancé's parents. A lot on. I'll go there myself in the next hour. What does the message say?'

Maggie told her.

'Send it to me. I'll get over to the parents and come to see you later. Mostly these troll efforts are just bluster. They threaten to kill you, rape you, but the perpetrator is all alone in his bedroom and couldn't burst a paper bag. I know that's not much comfort, but don't panic. I must go now, but we are on your case, Maggie.'

She rang off.

'Do you think she is?' said Maggie. 'Or is it just consoling words? The ones they tell everyone.'

'She is coming over,' he said. 'That's positive. Come downstairs. Talk to Judy. The more that know the better.'

Chapter 19

Jack left Maggie and Judy to sisterly support, listening in as much as he could as he set to work getting the damaged cupboards off the walls. They had been emptied, the contents on the various worktops and the kitchen island. The doors were all off, the shelves taken out, stacked on the patio.

He went out to his van, and took out his small step ladder. Somewhere in there, buried under the buckets, tools, wood that might come in useful, was a T-stand. He really must give the van a clear out. Would he ever use that sink?

The T-stand was one he'd made up when he was last working on kitchen cupboards, maybe five months ago. It consisted of a base, a pillar and a top crosspiece. Its function was to support the old cupboard as the screws were being taken out, so it wouldn't fall, ripping the plaster. It meant one person could handle the job.

Judy said she would help but she was busy with Maggie, saying much the same things that he and Nova had said from what he caught of it. Maggie didn't seem much comforted.

What could you say? Tell her it was bluster, when you didn't know who was sending the vile stuff was hardly comforting. Maybe changing the locks wasn't a waste of time and money, as who knows who it was and why. Best be safe.

Work was good for thinking. He often had his best ideas while sawing or chiselling. No one to interrupt.

Jack found the T-stand. It was exactly 50 centimetres high, a common height for cupboards above worktops. Too high and people, women especially, couldn't reach the top shelves.

He set to work on the first cupboard. It was a shell, door off, shelves removed, broken at the bottom and sides. He grimaced at the damage, deliberately done, so he could work. A crime to solve a crime. Well, not so far, he was clueless, finding motives for everyone in the house, plus Lily and Uncle Alec who had left, moaning that he couldn't even get a sandwich when Judy suggested that he go to Prèt á Manger.

The T-stand placed under the cupboard, he climbed three steps of the ladder, and with his electric screwdriver removed the holding screws, that were either side at top rear within the cupboard. The screws secured the cupboard to flat brackets screwed into the wall. Routine stuff.

Securing screws out, the cupboard rested on the tiny ledge of the brackets and the T-stand. He came off the ladder, lifted the cupboard off the brackets and brought it down to the worktop, feeling like a conjuror, having performed his ace trick. But no one was watching. Judy and Maggie still in sister-support mode. Appreciation or not, there were six cupboards on this side to come down and six more on the other side of the kitchen. Eleven to go.

What stupidity. Wrecked so he could replace them with the same. All before the wedding. It was like digging holes and filling them in again.

Jack took the cupboard shell out to the patio. It wasn't that heavy, but he had needed the T-stand while doing the unscrewing, as he only had two hands. On the patio, he bashed out the sides with a club hammer. Normally, he would be more protective. But the cupboard pieces were going to be sliced and chipped, mixed with resin, and compressed to become chipboard. So damage to the wood didn't matter in the slightest. He could swipe as hard as he liked with the club hammer. Get out his ill-humour.

Jack had taken down three cupboards when Nova arrived, and was working on another. He worked more slowly, wanting to hear what she had to say.

'I've been to Mo Bukhari's parents,' she said to Maggie and Judy. 'They deny any knowledge of threatening emails.'

'They would, wouldn't they,' said Maggie.

'Clearly they don't like you, saying that you bewitched their son, but deny any involvement in the emails.'

'What else would they say,' said Maggie. 'We dunnit, here's the evidence. No way. I hope you gave them a good scare.'

'We did our best,' said Nova. 'I went into the house with two uniformed officers. Big, beefy guys. Always scary. They certainly scare me. I made it clear to the Bukharis that anyone sending death threats would get a prison sentence. And if they got someone else to send them, all would be jailed. Mr Bukhari insisted it was all rubbish, that was the word he used. Though he wants nothing to do with the pair of you. I had two sons, now I have one, he said.'

'He's said that before,' said Maggie. 'Same old tune. And lying through his back teeth. He's out to get me killed.'

'We are going to keep a watch on this house,' said Nova. 'Drive past, call in every so often. And on the day of the wedding, we'll have a policeman here all day.'

'And after the wedding?' said Maggie. 'The rest of my life? What then?'

Jack was on the stepladder, halting the screwdriver to hear Nova's reply. Obviously, she couldn't offer lifetime protection.

'Let's take it to the end of your wedding day,' she said, 'and then decide what to do.'

A safe answer. He guessed that would be the end of police protection. Trolls so rarely follow through on their threats. But occasionally they do. Maggie and Nova were at opposite ends of the likelihood spectrum. Maggie's fear raising it to very likely, Nova's to slight chance, but just in case, she'd keep an eye on the house for a few days.

Though slight didn't mean never.

Nova came to Jack on his ladder.

'Let's talk in the garden,' she said.

He put down the electric screwdriver and followed her outside, over the patio and onto the centre of the lawn. He didn't like this. It selected him as having a special relationship with her. Which he did, but didn't want it telegraphed.

'What do you think?' she said.

'I wish you wouldn't do this,' he said. 'Single me out.'

'Sorry, Jack. Just tell them, I still think you might have smashed up the kitchen.'

'Utterly untrue.'

'These emails have given you a let out.'

'And scared the life out of Maggie.'

'Who do you think sent them?'

He shrugged. 'The best guess is Mo's family, but I really have no idea.'

'And Richard Ffrench's murder, got any further with that?'

'No. Lots of suspects. He wasn't a pleasant man. I wish you could get me that draft will.'

'I tried, Jack. Honest. But legally I can't give it to you. Fayyad says no. If I did it anyway, and it got out that I had, I would lose my job.'

'Thanks for trying. We'd better get back inside as they'll be wondering what we are jabbering about.'

Chapter 20

Jack worked on. The plan was to get all the broken cupboards and shelves off the walls today, and out on the patio, where he'd break them up. Tomorrow they'd be carted off to the chipboard factory. Attaching the new cupboards would be easier than it normally would be, as the brackets were there, and could be reused.

Maggie went off to watch TV. She told them she couldn't concentrate to carry on with her music or even read a book. She wanted some silly quiz show or soap, or a slushy movie. Judy left, telling him she had a meeting, something to do with an event she was organising, leaving him alone in the kitchen. That was OK, a bit of peace; he could focus on the work in hand and not get involved in chatter. Much of which was circular, too little information.

Then again, chatter put him in the picture, helped him to know the family. But Judy was out, and Maggie was in no state to talk about anything but the emails. Who he needed to talk to was Mo and Tom, and they were both at work. So get the damaged cupboards down. But in truth, he should leave them till someone came. Just sit about, get busy when the family were here. They were only an excuse to keep him here investigating. Except Judy was getting in a state about the cupboards not getting done in time. Which was rich coming from the lady who had smashed them up.

So he worked on, getting them down. But not rushing. He reasoned, he would be finished in plenty of time. Too early, if he pushed it, then there'd be no reason for him to stay. Perhaps he should smash something. A window, a door or two?

Not his style. He had a murder to solve. The big problem was that it was two months ago. The room where it happened had been utterly sterilised. And any evidence the police had, they certainly wouldn't let him see. They had their killer, safely locked up.

Jack worked and thought. No distractions as he took down the damaged cupboards, one by one, and hammered them apart on the patio.

Deal with the present. Have the threatening emails anything to do with the murder? Was the murderer sending them? If so, why? Or had they nothing to do with the murder at all, and been sent by Mo's family because of his marriage to a non-Muslim English girl. If so, he hoped Nova had frightened them into inaction.

Honour killing, though, was emotional. Impervious to reason. If it was that at all. He had the uncomfortable feeling the case would stay unsolved, and Cliff would remain in jail. Jack had his suspects, but not a single clue pointing to anyone in particular.

He needed a pointer, something to drive him.

His thoughts were interrupted by a phone call. It was Alison, his ex, Mia's mother, head teacher in a primary school. Their marriage had broken up when his drinking got out of control. But they still had a relationship, bound together in parenting Mia.

'What can I do for you, Alison?'

'Our daughter is in a cell in West End Central police station. I have just been to see her.'

That was a blast from the blue.

'What on earth is going on?'

'Three girls, including Mia, superglued themselves to the railings at the entrance to Downing Street. No one was able to get in or out while they chanted about climate change. They even held up the Prime Minister, which delighted our daughter as you might imagine.'

'This is serious stuff.'

He had a vision of the three young women glued to the railings, including Mia, who hadn't said a word to him about it last night. Photos snapping, the media on hand. Urban theatre, Mia called it.

'Stupid, senseless,' said Alison. 'There's already lots of footage, press, mobile phone videos. She is likely to get a jail sentence. They had to bring in a special team to cut away the superglue. The police are keeping the girls in jail overnight. Tomorrow they go to City of Westminster Magistrates court where their case will be tried. And I can't be there, Jack. We have a school inspection, so I must be there. They will quiz me on the school strategy, making sure have we ticked all the boxes. These stupid shenanigans, they take up so much time and energy. I have to keep staff nerves down. Sorry, Jack, but it's down to you to go to the court. Are you working?'

'I am. With lots to do. A job with a tight timetable.' And getting tighter. He had no wish to go into detail. But was thinking tomorrow was a washout workwise, with court in the morning, jail visit to Cliff in the afternoon.

'Has she got a lawyer?'

'Yes. One of those pro bono lawyers, a climate change sympathiser, will be defending them. I've spoken to him. Nice chap, very young. He's not optimistic they'll get off with a fine.'

'What time is her case?'

'10 am. Can you be at the court?'

'There's not a lot I can do there. But I suppose I have to go. This is such a turn up. Out of the blue. There I was, working steadily away, thinking I have lots of time.'

'Our daughter is full of surprises. Wear a suit. You might get the chance to speak up for her, the lawyer says.'

'I'll be there.'

He couldn't see he had any other option. He hated wearing a suit, and it would likely make not the slightest difference.

'How is Mia?' he said.

'Quite chirpy,' said Alison. 'She is comparing herself to the suffragettes. Saying prison would be an interesting experience. I couldn't make her see sense. She'll have a prison record which she'll carry with her all her working life. I wish she'd never got involved with climate change. I agree we have to halt it, but direct action just means trouble. '

There was little Jack could say to that. His daughter was fervent for the cause. She had been arrested a couple of times on demos, but always got off. This one didn't look at all likely to go that way.

She'd be going to jail.

Chapter 21

Judy was annoyed that Jack had to go to court in the morning.

'You can't do anything for her,' she said. 'And it's her stupid fault.'

'I can be there. Support. I agree it's dumb of her, but I am not abandoning my daughter.'

'How will the work get done?'

She indicated the cupboards. Six had been taken down and smashed up, all of one side, blank spaces on the wall with ghostly outlines and the two top brackets for each cupboard. On the other side of the kitchen, the remaining cupboards were like the remnants of a ghost town.

'I'll get the rest down today,' he said. 'Then tomorrow, if I come in at 6 am, I'll let myself in; I've got front door keys, plenty of front door keys. I can work till 8.30 then head for the court. After we've seen Cliff, I'll get straight back and work all night if I have to.'

'I suppose there's no option,' she accepted, somewhat reluctantly. 'And how's the investigating, if you haven't forgotten? This...' her arm swept round the kitchen cupboards, 'was meant to be the ruse for you being here to investigate. And now it's become the main event.'

'This sort of work is OK, I can think while I'm working. I am getting the picture. I've met all the suspects bar Cliff, talked to most of them. I know the house. We are going to see Cliff tomorrow, I want to know about his confession. If he didn't do it, why confess?'

'I have asked him that,' she said, 'every time I visit, and when I phone him. And he just clams up.'

'I can but try,' he said. 'And I do have contacts in the local police force.'

Though he was not thinking of contacting Nova again. She still thought he was a likely candidate for smashing up the kitchen, let alone his confused relationship with her. But Fayyad, her boss, higher up the chain, Detective Inspector Fayyad Kamani in full, he might get more out of him, lacking the emotional baggage that bedevilled him with Nova.

'Keep on it,' she said. 'We are where we are. I'll let you get on with your work. And oh yes, it's Pizza Tuesday. For dinner, we order a stack of pizzas from Giovanna's, the whole family gets together, to catch up and argue. Do you want to be part of it?'

'Won't it be awkward, if it's just family?'

'They'll all see you working late, and I am sure would want to invite you. You get on well with Maggie. In fact, she loves you, in a manner of speaking. I get on with you, in an up and down way, Mo sides with Maggie, unless he gets jealous, so don't sit next to her, and Tom will be happy to have a good looking guy at the feast.'

'Do you dress up?'

'We do indeed. High heels and party gear. No one will expect you to. We have it in the sitting room, place mats and all on the dining room table. We still have enough decent china. No booze, not any more, it got too quarrelsome, but a range of non-alcoholic fake booze and juice.'

'I'd love to come. Won't have far to go, will I? Something to look forward to.'

'You can sit next to me,' she said. 'That's if you want to.'

She gave him an enticing look, forgiving him his trespasses, and creating a few more. He recalled the long smooch they'd had at his place, that might have gone further, had not Mia come in.

Powerful women attracted him.

He was a few steps up the ladder, screwdriver in hand, she below, one hand on the ladder. He reached down putting his hand on hers. Touch, warmth, need.

'This is a very public place,' he said.

'I wasn't thinking of taking my clothes off.'

'Pity.'

She laughed and drew away. 'I've things to do. And so have you.'

'Pity,' he repeated.

Maggie came into the kitchen.

'Have I interrupted something?' she said, looking at her sister then at Jack.

'Just a discussion about cupboards,' said Judy. 'And things.'

'It was the things I'd like to know more about,' she said.

'So would I,' said Jack.

Judy said nothing.

'And I need company,' said Maggie. 'I can't watch any more TV. I can't follow the plots, too many people and I'm thinking of the emails and wondering is that the end of them. And is he going to turn up one night with a hatchet. I need something to do. Something brainless.'

'How about we pot those pelargoniums?' said Judy.

'That's about my level.'

Judy took her sister into the garden. He watched them cross the lawn and go into the shed.

Work. Distraction over. Though not quite, as his head was full of possibilities, even as he unscrewed another cupboard. And his daughter, the mess she had got into, with jail the likely consequence. Too much to think about.

Chapter 22

Jack took down the cupboards, one by one, and knocked them apart with his club hammer on the patio. Late afternoon, he joined Maggie and Judy on the lawn for a light tea of cheese and tomato sandwiches and ice cream.

Laying flat out, he looked into the sky. Clear blue, it would be a great night for his telescope, the thought pushed away by cupboards, Mia and by Judy. His thoughts were taking him for a ride: murder, sex, work and family intermingled. You think you are in charge, but it is they who have the reins. He should be concentrating on the investigation. But he couldn't grasp anything. Too elusive, too many possibilities. Too much time had passed. And Judy and Mia kept intervening. Work was the easy bit.

He went back to work, and was taking the last cupboard down when Mo came into the kitchen. Judy and Maggie were in the garden.

'How's it going, Jack?'

'It's been an eventful day. You need to talk to Maggie.'

'Has she cancelled the wedding?' he said jokily.

'No. But there's a problem.'

'Tell me.'

'I can't. It's not my place.'

'You mean you know and she hasn't told me.' A hint of anger in his voice.

'I know a little,' he said. He knew a lot, but was downplaying his part. 'Talk to Maggie.'

'I most certainly will.'

Mo strode out into the garden.

Jack watched them as he worked. He shouldn't have said anything. But Mo was going to get there soon enough, with or without him. Mo was standing, the two on the grass sitting up. There were raised voices, mostly his. Maggie showing him her phone. Jack caught the odd words, enough to tell him that Mo was incensed that she hadn't phoned him. He couldn't hear any of Maggie's reply but knew it. She didn't want to worry him. But plainly, he felt it was his duty to be worried.

Now she was shouting. He caught, 'I'm the one being threatened.' And a little later, 'I'm the one they want to kill.'

He couldn't hear Judy but by her body language, she was trying to pacify the couple. It wasn't working. After more shouting from Mo, Maggie rushed into the house, her face streaming with tears.

She raced through the kitchen, exclaiming, 'He doesn't understand, he doesn't understand,' and was out the door.

The holding screws removed, Jack took down a cupboard. It needed breaking up on the patio, but he figured he'd leave that a while. Mo was having an animated conversation with Judy on the lawn. He caught the words, 'She should have phoned me!'

His manhood undermined. His wife-to-be had got death threats and she hadn't contacted him. It was male pride. Everyone knew but him.

Mo came into the kitchen.

He said, 'How come you took her to the police station.'

Jack stopped working. 'There was no one else who could go. Judy was waiting for the cupboards to be delivered. I was the only one free. I only took her there. She did all the talking. I didn't say a word.'

'Why didn't she phone me, Jack?'

'She thought you would come rushing back.'

'I would. Of course, I would.' He was striding about the kitchen in anguish. 'This could be my family making death threats and she doesn't call me.'

'She loves you, Mo.'

'I love her. You don't know how much I love her.' His eyes were welling.

'Go and apologise.'

'But she didn't phone me, Jack. What does that say about our future life together?'

'She has been scared to death all day. Go and apologise.'

'But she didn't call me.'

'You can say that a hundred times. And it's true. But it's no help at all. You'll spend the next couple of days not talking to each other, both waiting for the other to apologise. She's just as mad at you as you are at her. Go and apologise.'

'Would you?'

Oh, big question. Too big a question. He could be as childish as the next man.

'Apologise for having a go at her. And she'll apologise to you, I bet you.'

'You think so?'

'She loves you, Mo. She wants to marry you. Just say sorry.'

Mo shook Jack's hand.

'Oh thank you, man. You speak so much sense. I am a fool. The craziest of crazy fools. She is the love of my life and I was yelling at her. She gets death threats from my family and I am yelling at her.'

'Go and apologise.'

Mo rushed off.

'Thank you, man. Thanks a million, you have saved my life!'

Jack took a drink of water. Such hard work being an agony aunt. You never know whether you'll be thanked or get a punch on the nose. So much easier to take down cabinets.

He'd developed some savvy on human nature from going to Alcohol Halt, the sessions for alkies, where he'd learnt, or rather been told by Max, the convener, that adults behave like children, they just pretend they are grown ups. In that circle of sinners, they certainly were a bunch of kids, in hock to booze, treating everyone around them badly, like the bully in the playground.

The trick, said Max, is to learn to apologise. Say sorry to everyone you have hurt through booze. Blessed are the meek. Learn to back down. Jack had questioned meekness. You don't want to get walked over. Max conceded that. There's a balance, he said. Which could be seen as a cop out, but then who has all the answers?

Jack had simply told Mo to apologise, and he was treating it like advice from God. Maybe because he knew he should.

Chapter 23

With all the cupboards down, Jack did some plastering. Here and there, lumps had been knocked out in Judy's wild dance with the hammer. The plaster would need to dry, but this was quick-dry plaster so would be fine by tomorrow. He'd need to sandpaper so the new plaster merged smoothly into the rest of the wall, then paint.

All simple, all logical, unlike the investigation. Though getting the exact colour might be a problem. The white paint on the wall had aged, while his would be fresh out of the can. A complete paint job was the sure fire remedy but there was no time for that. Especially with tomorrow's work time hedged in with court and a jail visit. It was the small jobs very often that held you up. They could be trickier than you realised.

He said to Judy, 'What if I don't finish?'

She looked at him aghast.

'Eighty people are coming to the wedding. I am not having every one of them saying, what's happened to your kitchen, Judy. With me having to say we had an intruder and Maggie joining in and saying it was Mo's family. Just get it done, please, Jack.'

'It'll happen,' he said, not absolutely sure how, with him out the house much of tomorrow. But there were twenty-four hours in a day, and who needs sleep.

Judy had seated herself at the island, and, with a menu before her, was ordering the pizzas. His stomach rumbled as she went through her list. Italian titles for the pizzas with Judy adding extra mushrooms, no anchovies, more olives.

Quite a feast. The pizzas ordered, she marched out of the room with a table cloth and cutlery.

He noted she seemed to be doing all the setting up. But then Judy was one of those people only happy when they are busy. He would bet she'd had the idea for pizza night for something to do.

Tom came in, still wearing his Peaky Blinders hat and red silk scarf. Jack wondered what his workplace was like. All like that or did Tom stand out?

'What have you done to our kitchen, Jack?'

That was hardly a joke, considering what Nova thought of his actions.

'Cupboards and shelves go up tomorrow. Then I paint the fresh plaster.'

'It's going to look a little patchy.'

'Not with my colour matching.' Said with a confidence, he didn't quite have.

Tom came in closer. 'Judy tells me Maggie and Mo had a row, but wouldn't say what about. Have you heard anything?'

Jack considered how much to tell him, as Judy wasn't giving him the details. But he needed to get Tom talking. He'd risk her wrath.

'Maggie got some threatening emails,' he said. 'And called the police, but didn't phone Mo. And he got very angry when he got in and found out.'

'What did the emails say?'

Tom was pouring himself some orange juice, the colour went well with his scarf.

'You're dead if you marry Mo. Something like that,' said Jack.

'Wow! Heavy stuff.' He threw back the juice. 'I'll go up and see her.'

He turned to depart, but Jack called him back.

'I wouldn't, if I were you. Mo and Maggie are making up. Or let's hope they are.'

'Wouldn't do to interrupt,' said Tom with a smirk. 'I'll get the full story over dinner.'

Jack saw the chance to quiz Tom further.

'The police think it might be connected with your father's murder.'

He threw that in, knowing the police didn't think that at all, having Cliff in jail. But he needed to bring up the murder to get Tom's views on it.

'That doesn't make sense,' said Tom. 'Unless they are having doubts that Cliff is the killer.'

'What do you think?'

'They've got the wrong person. The fuzz do that all the time, then never admit they have made a mistake. A group cover-up, they defend each other to the ends of the earth. Cliff is no killer. Who did it I don't know, but frankly, I am glad that Dad is no more. Let's not be prissy. Dead.'

'That's a heavy thing to admit. Especially about your father.'

'Does that make me the killer, Jack?' He laughed, as if telling a secret.

'From what I hear, not many people liked your dad.'

'Find me one.'

'Lily says she misses him.'

Tom waved a disparaging hand. 'We all know what Lily was up to. She wanted a big slice of the business and reckoned she could get that in bed. But that didn't quite work out for her. She got some, but feels cheated. One of Dad's mean tricks. In the bedroom, I am sure he was promising her the world and the moon. That was Dad all along. As a kid I can imagine him pulling the legs off spiders and tying tin cans to cats' tails. As a grown up, he picked on those around him. He insulted me daily. I had to move back here when I lost my flat. Some bad advice from my stockbroker. Being gay is not enough of a reference for a financial advisor, let me tell you.'

Tom laughed. 'Dad wanted me to have anti gay treatment, said he'd pay for the best. Read worst. I said, what about giving me the money instead. But no, it was just for a charlatan who would give me drugs and tell me how, in a hundred ways, being queer was against God and nature.'

'Uncle Alec lectured me on how Mr Ffrench had ripped him off.'

'Uncle Alec hasn't exactly got clean hands.' He came in close, almost overpowering Jack with his perfume. 'You are learning all our secrets, Jack.'

'It's working in the kitchen,' he said. 'Everyone comes in.'

'Tell me one of your secrets. So we can gossip about you. Something juicy. Fair's fair.'

Jack thought for a few seconds. He had to give something.

'I proposed to my girlfriend a few days ago,' he said. 'In the Himalaya restaurant. I had the ring ready, when she told me she was going with someone else. A woman.'

Tom clapped his hands and laughed. 'Classic!'

'Painful,' he said, feeling belittled.

'Sorry, Jack, but I have been dumped myself too often. I have to make a joke of it or I'll break down in tears. And now I must get ready for our pizza party. You should come. We can't leave you starving in the kitchen like Cinderella, all alone while the family are at the ball.'

'Judy invited me.'

'You more than deserve it. Must have a shower and put my glad rags on. You look fine. I like a bit of rough.' He blew him a kiss. 'Come as you are. And you may well learn some more secrets.'

He left with a wave.

A few minutes later, Judy was back in the kitchen collecting crockery. Jack was surprised how much of it they still had, considering how much had been broken. He offered to help with the fetching and carrying.

'Stick to your task.' She gave him a peck on the cheek. 'Did you get much out of Tom?'

'He hated your dad.'

'Tell me someone who didn't.' He was about to say Lily, but Judy was out the room with a pile of plates.

Chapter 24

Judy came in to call him for dinner. She was wearing a red dress, with matching lipstick, a fair, or unfair amount depending on your viewpoint, of cleavage, red high heels and a yellow ribbon in her hair.

'Have you a dresser and a make up artist hidden in your room?'

'I had everything laid out, ready and waiting.'

She was so enhanced from her workaday self, he was overawed.

'I need a fairy godmother to match you.'

'Prince Charming has another gig. You will have to fill in. It's fancy dress. You can come as a builder.'

Not a detective, with deerstalker and magnifying glass.

He could hardly look at her, she was so hot. It was unfair. She blew him away.

'Come on.' She took his arm.

'I must finish this plastering,' he said indicating the bucket of daub, 'or it'll go off. Be ten minutes.'

He could see she was reluctant to let him stay in the kitchen, her beau for the ball. Though he felt quite unappealing. Much as he wanted to join her, she was intimidating, so dolled up.

She looked about the room, what he'd done, what was still to be done.

'Ten minutes,' she said. 'And not one second longer.'

She left the kitchen, leaving Jack half relieved and half regretful. It would be twitchy, the pizza party with all the family there, all dressed to the nines, if she was anything to go by, and he in paint stained jeans and a matching flecked

T-shirt. He could do with a shave, and have more suitable footwear than boots. He daren't take them off with a hole in one heel. Still, they'd be under the table.

Dressing up was not his thing. He'd have to wear a suit for court tomorrow. That always felt like a straitjacket, as if he'd be on trial and not his daughter.

The thought cooled his hormones. She could be jailed.

But the plaster was thickening. Deal with now. He wanted to get all the damage to the wall done, so the plaster would be completely set by tomorrow. Quick dry was no miracle, just overnight rather than days. And then the cupboards, the shelves too, grouting at the cupboard edges, somehow finding time in a crowded day to do it all, what with Mia's court case and the visit to Pentonville jail.

Sufficient unto the day are the evils thereof, as his mother would say, Matthew something or other. Sound advice. Not that it ever stopped him worrying.

Jack smeared plaster on the dents and cracks, until he'd covered all the war wounds. The remnant was in a throwaway bucket. Best not tell Mia, reminding him once again she was in a cell at West End Central. Cross fingers for tomorrow.

Plastering done, he went to the kitchen sink and washed his hands and face, wiping himself on paper kitchen towel. His hair could do with a comb, but he hadn't one. It would hardly make any difference, all considered.

Straightening himself, breathing steadily, trying to appear confident, he went into the dining room.

The room was darkened, the curtains closed, dancing shadows from four tall candles on the dining table, the only light. The table was laid out with six pizzas. On a trolley nearby were jugs of juice and bottles of non-alcoholic beverages with a range of glasses.

Just Tom and Judy were at the table, competing in colour. He wore a yellow Peaky Blinders cap with red silk scarf over a blue T-shirt, his arms tanned and muscular, tattoos of Chinese dragons down both.

Some jazz was quietly playing.

He went to take a seat by Judy.

'Not there,' she said sharply. 'That's Cliff's place. The other side.' She tapped the seat in case he was unsure.

Jack had almost sat in the reserved seat, for the man who wasn't coming. There were family rituals here. He sat on her other side, engulfed in her perfume. Tom was across from him.

'No Maggie and Mo?' said Jack.

'They'll be down,' said Judy. 'I went up ten minutes ago to remind them. They have been making up and, you know, got somewhat delayed.' She flapped a hand to indicate what had kept them. 'Got a little preoccupied, let's say. Help yourself, Jack.'

The pizzas had been cut into slices. He hardly knew where to start, they were so enticing. Six pizzas, he noted. One for Cliff? He would not ask. Besides which, they were all for sharing.

'Fill your plate, Jack,' said Tom. 'You are our special guest.'

'Let me make you up a cocktail,' she said. 'Non alcoholic. The hard stuff is banned.'

She went to the trolley, and taking a tall glass began filling it with various coloured liquids.

'How come booze is banned?' he said, not wanting any himself, being an alkie, or ex alkie depending on his will power or lack of it, but assuming the other diners weren't teetotal.

Tom laughed. 'Mo and I got in our cups and had a fight. First of these dinners. I can hardly remember what over.'

'Paddington Bear,' said Judy. 'Of all things. Can you believe it. Two grown men slugging it out over a stuffed toy.'

She gave Jack his cocktail.

'That was it, Paddington, so stupid,' exclaimed Tom. 'Mo was saying he was utterly marvellous, the films wonderful, and I was saying it was a triumph of marketing over substance. A bear from deep darkest Peru speaking perfect English and eating marmalade sandwiches. When I told him it was just a kids' toy, he went for me.'

'And we banned alcohol after that,' said Judy.

Booze makes you stupid, he knew well enough.

'This is delicious,' said Jack sipping the cocktail. 'What's in it?'

'Your five a day. Orange, blueberry, elder, lime and peach.'

'The healthiest cocktail I've ever had.'

'Did you know Mo and Maggie share a bed with Paddington?' said Tom.

He did, but attempted surprise.

'On no account criticise him, the bear I mean,' added Tom. 'He is the holy grail. Unless you want a black eye.'

'I don't have strong feelings about Paddington Bear,' he said.

'Neither do I,' said Tom with a wink. 'I was just winding him up.'

'And very drunk,' added Judy.

Mo and Maggie came in. Tom smirked but the topic was over.

Mo was in a smart navy suit, a light blue shirt and navy tie. Surprisingly formal. He reminded Jack of Nova in her working gear. Maggie had stuck to jeans, somewhat figure hugging. It would take a paring knife to get them off. She had an orange frilly top, a rainbow headband, and purple lipstick.

He felt ultra dull with this show of colour and glam.

'Whose idea was it to have pizza parties?' he said, pretty sure who.

'Mine,' said Judy, confirming his intuition. 'Dad had just died. I had moved back here, so had Maggie with Mo. Cliff, well you know about Cliff, and where he is. I thought let's have one night when the whole house gets together.'

'To commemorate Dad's passing. Ha ha,' said Maggie.

'To celebrate the death of a homophobe,' said Tom.

'I wish we could just talk football,' said Mo. 'Or films, or books or how about the food.'

At the trolley, Mo was making up drinks for Maggie and himself.

'It's not everyone has a father who gets murdered,' said Tom.

'Lucky us,' said Maggie.

'Didn't he cut you all out of his will?' said Jack, knowing he hadn't, but correctives could be revealing.

'He was about to,' said Tom. 'We were all for the work-house, in a manner of speaking.'

'And I thought advertising paid well,' said Maggie. 'That shows how little I know.'

'Stealing from the poor, that's the spirit of advertising,' said Tom. 'Mind you, there are some in my firm who believe the world wouldn't spin unless it was advertised.'

'But you are the firm's sceptic,' said Mo.

'Yes, I think it has something to do with gravity.'

'The moon is slowing the earth down,' said Jack, with recent knowledge culled from his astronomy mag. 'Because of the tides. Two milliseconds every hundred years.'

'Something else to worry about on top of climate change,' said Maggie.

'In 200 million years, we'll have a 25 hour day.'

'And get the same pay for it,' said Tom. 'The sharks.'

The dinner was well underway. They were helping themselves to slices of pizza and going to the drinks trolley.

'Did you hear about those three women who locked themselves to Downing Street railings?' said Mo. 'What was the point of that?'

Jack hadn't realised it had made the news. He felt the need to defend his daughter. Just as well booze was banned.

'Climate change is the biggest calamity facing the human race,' he said. 'But most people don't care. And if we don't care, neither will the government.' A direct quote from Mia. 'Sorry, but my daughter is one of the three women.'

'A rebel in the family,' said Tom. 'Good luck to her, I say.'

'But what good will it do,' said Mo. 'With respect, Jack. She'll get a criminal record, and nothing will change.'

'If no one spoke up,' said Judy, 'nothing will change.' She stroked his thigh under the table.

'It all comes down to who has the best copy,' said Tom. 'Though it's hard to beat, nothing will change, doom doom doom, what's the point.'

'Give me some good copy,' said Jack.

'Let me think, let me think.' He scratched his chin, in a mock thinking pose.

'You've got him going now, Jack. Super advertiser on his way to save the Planet!'

Tom clicked his fingers. 'Got it.' He paused for their attention. 'Historians' right to work.'

The others contemplated this.

'Don't get it,' said Mo.

Maggie nudged him. 'If we are all doomed then historians will have no work.'

Mo brushed it away, 'Too damned clever. It has to be simple.'

'So even you will understand it,' said Tom.

'Run away and play, Tom,' said Maggie.

'Can we all back off,' said Judy. To Jack, 'We are not always so petty.'

'Just sometimes,' said Maggie.

'Could be advertisers' right to work,' said Tom contemplating, 'or TV executives for that matter, but I agree it's too subtle. Needs to be harder hitting, more straightforward.'

'See how they work,' said Maggie. 'All round the table, all those Oxbridge graduates, throwing in two penn'orth of genius.'

'I don't think advertising slogans will save the planet,' said Jack.

'Neither do I,' said Tom.

'Can I quote you on that,' said Maggie. 'Such an admission.'

'Don't sound so surprised, my little sister. Advertisers are part of the problem. Persuading people to buy what they don't want. Filling up the landfill sites, junking the seas. Mea culpa, my friend and my family.'

'Enough on that topic,' said Judy. 'Jack is going to court tomorrow morning to support his daughter, so he doesn't need our jokes.'

'Sorry, mate,' said Mo. 'I was out of order. I hope she gets off.'

'I back that,' said Tom. 'Tell her the world needs all the climate rebels it can get. In fact,' he clicked his fingers, 'we have guest speakers once a month, can she speak?'

'Can a cow moo,' said Jack.

'We'll book her. If I can persuade management. They like to be insulted. Tell her to bash the advertising industry into next week. She'd get paid, of course.'

Jack thanked him. Mia might take up the offer, if she was out of clink. He liked Tom, but wondered how he got on at work, being so contrary to its ethics.

Judy rapped the table with her spoon.

'We can't evade the elephant in the room.'

They all looked to her. Jack helped himself to a slice of mushroom pizza. He'd like more of the cocktail Judy had made up but would have to wait to ask her, now she had the table.

'The threatening emails,' she said. 'Death threats to our Maggie. What are we going to do about them, what can we do?'

'The police are going to watch the house,' said Mo.

'Once a day,' said Maggie disdainfully.

'The locks have been changed,' said Tom. 'So the vandal can't get in again.'

Jack had wondered how long it would take to bring the vandal/intruder in. Two fifty plus on locks, not counting his time.

'We need a burglar alarm,' said Mo.

'That'll take weeks to be put in, darling,' said Maggie, patting his wrist. 'But now, what can we do now. That's what matters.'

'What do you think, Jack,' said Judy.

'Find out who is doing it,' he said, 'and stop them.'

'That's rather like the mice saying let's bell the cat,' said Tom. 'Easier said than done.'

'Agreed,' said Jack, but he was mulling it over.

There had been no intruder, he and Judy knew that for sure. But there were email threats, they were utterly real. Which may or may not be actioned. It had to be someone who knew the kitchen had been smashed up, as the first said, 'Second Warning', as if claiming the smashing of the kitchen as one of its warnings.

'Can you make me more of that cocktail, Judy,' he asked. 'I'd try it myself, but I'm sure I'd just make some awful gloop.'

'Delighted to.'

He was feeling weighty. Best eat no more.

They talked over security for Maggie. She shouldn't go out alone, bolts for the back door, order a burglar alarm.

But he was going to bell the cat.

Chapter 25

Jack had gone back to the kitchen, leaving the others talking burglar alarms, the hassle of having to set one every day, and having a strict minute to turn it off when you came back in, with the right codes, or it would blast away, unstoppable until an operative arrived. The cops never ever came, with so many false alarms.

They'd called Jack back as he left them to work on, telling him tomorrow was another day. It surely was, but filled up with lots of non work. He wanted to get some of the cupboards up tonight. Each was a flat pack that had to be assembled. He would assemble each one without the doors on, making it easier to put them up.

Taking the first one out of its cardboard box, he had a quick read of the instructions. If there were any problems, it would be on the first. He examined what was in there. Two sides, top and bottom, back, doors, all there. He put the doors aside and looked at the fittings, ignoring the door hinges and the brackets and screws for attaching to the wall. He was only interested in the items for fitting the cupboard together. Helpfully, they had their own little pack: small wooden plugs that held the four sides together along with glue, not included, that he had himself. More or less stand-ard.

His stomach was feeling somewhat bloated. You don't work after a big meal, if you could help it. Normally just a sandwich or two at lunch. Though sometimes tempted by a fry up at the local cafe. But tonight, he had definitely over-done the pizzas, sampling each of them, along with three cocktails.

He'd work it off.

Measuring up, he did the drilling, and assembled the first cupboard with plugs and glue. That was straightforward, well, had to be, as the company had to have a system for the assemblage of their flatpacks, being done by amateurs, as well as professionals, across the land.

The bloating was growing. Should he ask for some stomach tablets? No, work on. It would go, though it was quite a pain, and causing him to belch. His weakness, lack of self-control, he should have known when to stop eating.

Halfway though assembling the second cupboard, it was too much, he was going to be sick. He rushed to the downstairs toilet, stuck his fingers down his throat to hurry things along, and vomited pizza and cocktails into the toilet bowl.

Jack stayed on his knees for half a minute, but he was already feeling better, the pressure off his guts. He cleaned up the toilet with loo paper, pulling the handle several times to flush it all away. Then washed himself.

Much better. He shouldn't pig himself like that, as if he'd never seen pizzas before. In the kitchen, he gargled away the sour taste.

All done, evidence flushed away. No one would know the effects of his gluttony.

Jack went back to work, slowly at first, but getting back to pace. He was returning to health, and hoped he could get three cupboards assembled and up on the wall tonight. Tomorrow, he'd come in at 6 am, and do as much as he could before he had to leave for court.

The four diners came in with plates and cutlery, Judy pushing the trolley of juices and pretend booze. He was relieved he'd got the vomiting over and done with half an hour ago, and not humiliated himself in front of the family.

Jack was complimented on the two cupboards he had assembled, while they put food scraps in the bin, filled the dishwasher and the fridge. They were well organised, not surprising as this task had become a weekly routine. Maggie was wrapping leftovers in cling film, and the others filling the dishwasher. And in a good mood too with their team work, no punches thrown. A very colourful group of scullery lads and lasses.

Maggie was concerned at Jack continuing working.

'You can't work all night,' she said. 'It's against all health and safety and whatever rules.'

'I am getting well paid,' he said.

'Even so. There has to be a limit.'

'Let's say, it is my wedding present to you and Mo. The kitchen restored to life, so none of your guests will even know anything happened.'

'While you die of overwork.'

'I'll survive,' he said.

They left him. All but Judy, still dazzling in her red dress and yellow ribbon.

She said, 'Do you want to stay the night?'

A little unsure what was on offer, he said:

'On the sofa?'

'No,' she said. 'In a warm bed.'

'Will I get much sleep?'

'That's up to you.'

They looked at each other, which was assent enough, but fully confirmed by an embrace. Welcome warmth and fervency. In the kitchen amidst new cupboards, a swishing dishwasher the music of their embrace. Enclosed in arms, the press of bodies, lips sealing each other's promise.

When they broke up, she said, 'I must get out of this dress. It's too tight with all I've eaten. Then we'll have a hot chocolate and talk about tomorrow. Then bed.'

She was away.

Quite a whirlwind was Judy. He hoped he could keep up with her tempo.

He finished assembling the third cupboard. Quite an evening, with lots to think about if he could keep his head straight. Belling the cat, his tag for finding the email troll, his daughter in court, visit to Cliff who he'd only ever heard about, and bed with the belle of the ball.

And vomiting in the toilet.

What goes in, must come out, one way or another.

Judy was longer than he thought she'd be. Vomiting too? Surely not. Though bodies could only be disabused so much. He preferred to think of her in her red dress and yellow ribbon. Forget body's treachery.

She returned in jeans and T shirt.

'I've had a rethink, Jack. There's so much on tomorrow, and I'm feeling rather bloated. I've a list as long as my arm, and what with visiting Cliff too, plus you have a crowded agenda. Going to court and all the work to be done in here. I don't think we should sleep together. Not tonight, not the way my stomach is rebelling. I hope you don't mind.'

Chapter 26

Jack assembled three cupboards, with doors and shelves to go in once they were up. So march on. He attached each cupboard to the wall with the aid of his T support as a third hand. It was easier than it might have been, as the brackets from the last lot were still in place, so the cupboards only required screwing into them.

Work, a remedy of sorts, to cover disappointment. Better though if it had never been on offer. She blew hot, blew cold. Then again, her stomach was acting up. He knew all about that, but felt as lonely as a flagpole.

Work.

Not booze. Ever. Just as well they didn't keep it in the kitchen, as it was the sure fire remedy for all loss and loneliness, blotting out the world and its ills. Till you woke, and everything was worse.

The three cupboards up. He stood back. A quarter of them. Just put on the doors and put in the shelves, and then it would be a proper quarter. So he set to it. First the three doors, a little measuring to work out exactly where the hinges would go. You wouldn't want a lopsided door.

It was nearly eleven o'clock when Jack put in the last shelf. Satisfying, but then reminded of the destruction, how he was simply replacing what had already been there. Depressing, in time wasted, in all that lovely wood thrown away, and nine cupboards still to go up, to get back to where they were two days ago.

Time to go home before he depressed himself into the grave. Get out of this house. Get some sleep before he was due back again. A quick tidy of his tools, they could be left for the morning. Leave. He didn't want to encounter Judy again, or any human for that matter, as he was utterly weary in mind and body.

The TV was on in the TV room as he passed, likely they were all there. He could have put his head round the door and said his goodbyes, but Judy would have no doubt seen him to his van and he couldn't face that. He'd had enough of her for one night.

Or rather not enough.

Quietly, he opened the front door, stepped out into the night and closed it gently behind him. It was dark with a hint of twilight in the midsummer sky. The curtains were closed in the TV room with a slight spillage of light.

He walked down the path to his van, freer in the open air. The sky was clouded over, not a good night for stargazing. Not that he felt like it, too knackered, it had been an early start and a late finish. He hoped he could sleep with his jumble of thoughts: Mia, Judy, the work, the investigation. The latter had stalled, with all the work in the kitchen. He had suspects but no pointers as to whom.

Jack drove home, he could have walked it in fifteen minutes, but weariness plonked him in the van seat. A three minute drive, with little traffic. He was able to park outside his house. As he alighted, there came a call from across the road.

'Jack!'

He knew the voice, knew the silhouette. Nova. She was barely visible in her navy blue suit, just her face and blonde hair catching a little of the lamplight.

What on earth did she want? He was tired of women. Of rejection. He would like to be on a desert island with nothing but a telescope.

'I was passing,' she said, coming over.

He thought, she must have been waiting some time. Unlikely, she had come just as he'd arrived.

'Are you going to arrest me?' he said, holding wrists out for the cuffs.

She waved a dismissive hand. 'That's history. The threatening emails blur the likelihood that you damaged the kitchen. Unless you sent them.'

He laughed.

'You really have it in for me.'

'I have been mean to you, Jack.'

He shrugged. 'Being a detective makes you mean. I get it.' Thinking of the role he was playing and lies he was telling. 'I assume this is not a social call?'

'No. I can give you some help with the murder of Richard Ffrench.'

Much as he wanted to go straight to bed, to lose himself in sleep, there was no choice but hear what she had to say.

'You'd better come in,' he said.

Upstairs in the flat, Jack made tea. It seemed aeons since he'd been here in the morning, when he was someone else. The kitchen was as untidy as he had left it, the house fairies skipping his flat.

While he got tea things ready, she washed the dishes. He wasn't in a mood to say leave them. She had been pushing and prodding him for the last few days, so tea was the utter limit of his hospitality. And no apology for lack of biscuits.

Jack grinned at his pettiness. She had her back to him, her hands in the sink, so could not see. He would not apologise for the broken dishwasher.

Dishes done, tea poured out, he waited for her news. They were both at the table as they had been many times, though now separated by a chasm.

'We must learn to be friends,' she said.

'Difficult if you keep trying to arrest me.' He didn't bring up the event in the Himalaya restaurant. Prehistoric news.

'I don't know what I can do about that,' she said with a weak smile. 'I do think some weird things went on in that kitchen, but now it is all so confused what with the death threats that it would never stand up in court.'

'I am free to go.'

'But don't leave the country.'

They both laughed. Almost like old friends.

'I don't want us to be enemies,' she added.

'Me neither.'

Thought it would be some time before he could ask her out on the Flats with the telescope. If ever, now that she had a new partner, whom he had no wish to meet.

'I can tell you about the draft will,' she said, 'on the condition, you haven't heard it from me. Agreed?'

This was a turnabout. She was seriously trying to build bridges.

'Agreed.'

'It's written in awful legalese as these things are, but I'll give you the essence. I refreshed myself on the contents just an hour ago.' She took a deep breath, and continued. 'Uncle Alec has his ten percent of the business but would get no addition in the draft will. The children, that's Cliff, Maggie, Tom and Judy, would get 5% each. But the bulk of the business, that's 70%, would go to Lily.'

'70% to Lily!' he exclaimed. 'To the housekeeper?' That knocked him back. 'I know she was sleeping with him, but however you read it, that would have been one dirty trick on his children.' He reflected. 'I shouldn't be surprised from all I've heard about Richard Ffrench. But something puzzles me. It doesn't quite fit.' He struggled to put his suspicions into words. 'If Lily gets the lion's share, I am surprised he was going to give his children anything at all.'

Children, what else could you call grown up offspring, kids, sprogs. To be sent to bed without any supper.

'Fayyad and I discussed it,' she said. 'It is a puzzle. If he was going to give most of his business shares to his house-keeper to punish his children, why not give her all of his shares? That would teach them, whatever he wanted to teach them.'

'What a mean old curmudgeon he was.'

'But he could be yet meaner. This is what me and Fayyad settled on. If he gave the kids nothing, they would be resentful but be out of the business. Not going to meetings, or getting minutes and accounts, not voting at the AGM. But if he gives them a small allotment, then Lily, their one time housekeeper, bosses it over them at shareholder meetings, when she signs important documents which they disagree with, and that is just too bad. For ever and ever. His payback for lack of respect, them not being what he wanted them to be.'

'But the draft will never got signed,' he said. 'The dirty deed wasn't done. Richard Ffrench was killed first.'

'His children got their legacies on the terms of the existing will. Currently, each of them have a little over 20% each of the business, with Lily having only 5%. So it is she who has next to no say.'

Jack was mulling it over. Trying to get into Richard Ffrench's head. A man who wanted to be remembered at any cost. A sort of Hitler complex. Except he didn't know he was going to die.

'His new will was to show them who was boss,' said Jack. 'Do what I say and I might change it. If you all kowtow long enough.'

'There's more. It's hard to get to grips with.' She shuddered, and shook her hands as a show of her feelings. 'In the draft will, the house too was going to Lily.'

Jack blew out his cheeks. 'That is one hell of a bombshell. Not only would Lily have the business, but she can evict the kids or charge them sky high rent to stay in the house. Her house. The one where she has been the cleaner for years.' A wry thought struck him. 'Do you think he was a secret communist?'

She laughed.

'Equality was not in his vocabulary.'

So much to take in. Lily would have got the lot. Shares and his house. Nova had ignited Jack up with the surprise of it. Tiredness banished in an adrenaline rush. And he wasn't a beneficiary. He could imagine the earthquake to come if the will had been signed. After their father's death, Maggie, Judy,

Cliff and Tom go to the solicitor's office. He'd have Lily there too. And the solicitor read out the contents.

They would want to kill Lily, the four of them, with a paperknife.

'What's your thinking, Jack?'

'Beyond the fact their old man was a bastard?'

'We'll take that as read.'

'Judy, Cliff, Tom and Maggie have the best motives for murder,' he said, 'but only, if one of them knew what was in the draft will.'

'Richard Ffrench did have a paper copy, with a number of scratching outs. Minor adjustments. CSI found it in his room, post murder. It is possible one of the children saw it.'

'You think Cliff.'

'We do. And there has been a development there too.'

More. She was delivering tonight. He could almost forgive her, though there was an an abundance of love and hate locked in that 'almost'.

'Just this afternoon,' she went on, 'we have been informed that Cliff Ffrench has withdrawn his confession.'

Chapter 27

Nova left. He went with her to her car, thanking her. Perhaps they could be friends. And if he was going to be any sort of private investigator, he told himself, he would need friends in the police force. Although meeting Nova, or simply talking on the phone, pained him. But she at least had made the effort, and could get in trouble if she were revealed as his source.

She wouldn't be, not by him at least.

Before going to bed, he scrawled a few notes, which he hoped would make sense in the morning, as it wouldn't do to get things muddled:

Draft will

Lily – 70 per cent of shares + the house

Kids – 5 per cent of shares each

& Cliff retracted confession

Tiredness returned. He had been wide awake with Nova here. Her presence and the bombshell of the draft will had shaken him into life. But she was gone, message delivered, and he was as empty as a spent firework.

A quick wash, cleaning his teeth in automaton mode, Jack went to bed, setting the alarm for 5.30 am.

But sleep wasn't easy, his thoughts like clothing tumbling in a washing machine. Lily and the draft will, the Ffrench offspring as prime suspects, his daughter going to jail, Judy, Nova, tumbling together in a wash of froth and maximum spin.

He'd managed maybe three hours sleep when the alarm went off. Yesterday, he slept in after the alarm, not today. Too much to do. Work, court, jail. He got up quickly, less he was tempted to turn over and sleep on.

Jack washed, cleaned his teeth and was out of the house. There was plenty to eat at the Ffrench house with all the leftover pizza, he'd fill up there. He had keys to the house. Everyone had a set bar Lily, must get a set to her, and that would be everyone. He'd kept a set for himself with Judy's agreement, and the spares and Lily's were in a drawer in the kitchen island.

He drove to the house, waking up on the way. It was light, the sky blue and cloudless, cool but could be hot later once the sun was up. No traffic to speak of.

Once parked, the car locked, he went down the path and let himself in quietly. The unlocking reminding him of all the waste. Locks that weren't needed, a kitchen smashed up so he could work. The futility to it all, which might be assuaged if he found the killer. The big, prodding if.

In the kitchen, the three completed cupboards greeted him, proudly up on the wall. He was glad he had stayed to put on the doors and fit the shelves. Three more cupboards this side to do, and six the other. Did they really need so many? Or a kitchen this size. Not for him to question. The client is the boss.

Work. Get on the move, and he'd have some breakfast in an hour.

Jack brought in three flatpacks from the hall. He knew the drill, the right fittings to build just the shell, with no shelves or door. He'd get these three assembled, ready to go on the wall, and eat. It was just 6 am, no one else awake in the house. So no interruptions likely for an hour or more. He would work till 8.30, go home and put on his suit, and then go off to the court.

It was while finishing the second cupboard that he felt wobbly, a little light headed. Too early for him, this tail end of a night shift. Working on, drilling and screwing, he had a vision of Nova and Maggie slugging it out. A fist fight, starting in the kitchen and going out into the garden, their arms held out straight like 19th century bare fist fighters.

Why those two?

Nova, well yes, she was always at the tip of consciousness, but Maggie?

She was shouting, 'Come on copper, threaten me and see what you get.'

'Come quietly,' said Nova, 'and I won't use the cuffs.'

It was utterly illogical. Nova was a black belt and would have floored Maggie before any punch landed. Except Maggie was getting the best of it and had given Nova a bloody nose. He wanted to cheer her on, but was unable to speak.

Why Maggie?

He heard someone say, 'there's blood, all that blood.'

Whose blood? Must be Nova's.

He opened his eyes. Tom and Lily were standing over him, concern on their faces. He tried to stand up.

'Get a chair, Lily,' said Tom.

Jack supported himself on the kitchen island, and got to his feet, shaky, groggy.

'Some orange juice, please,' he said to Tom. 'A big glass.'

Tom went to the fridge, Lily returned with a chair, and helped Jack sit in it.

'That's quite a cut,' she said. 'I'll get the first aid kit.'

Tom gave Jack a large orange juice. He drank it greedily, swilling some in his mouth. It was filling him, the sugary sweetness, like a mattress being blown up.

'What happened, Jack?'

'Stupid idiot,' he said, smiling thankfully at Tom, with his Peaky Blinders cap and scarf as if he'd been up all night. 'Diabetic collapse,' he added. 'I should have eaten.'

'Plenty of grub here,' said Tom. 'Will pizza do you?'

'Yes, please.'

He wondered how long he'd been out. He looked at his watch. 7.50. Must have been more than an hour. So much for getting in early.

Tom gave him a plate of four slices of pizza, some salad and more juice.

'That do you?'

'Plenty,' said Jack. 'You are a saint.'

'No one has ever called me that before,' he said with a grin. 'Least not in this house.'

Lily tended his cut forehead while he ate and drank, snipping off a little hair. He was coming back to life with the pizza and juice. He should have eaten as soon as he got here. Wise after the fact. So obvious. He could have had some juice before starting work, made up a plate of pizza slices and nibbled as he worked.

Too obvious.

'It's not as bad as it looks,' said Lily, wiping the cut. 'A gash to the forehead always bleeds a lot. It's clean now. I'll put on some antiseptic, and then bandage it up.'

'Do I really need a bandage?' he said, seeing himself standing in the witness box in court in a few hours time with a bandaged head. There to speak up for his daughter, looking like a prize fighter who had been KO'd.

'Yes,' said Lily. 'It's too big for a plaster.'

'Must leave you, my dears, early meeting,' said Tom. 'You are in good hands with Lily. And I can see you are almost back in the land of the living. Though I am surprised that, with all you ate last night, not that I was watching you, that you were quite so depleted in the morning.'

Jack had vomited up all that potential nourishment. He'd come in on empty. But had no wish to add overeating to his list of sins.

'Thanks for the nosh,' he said. 'I'm feeling much better. I could sing the National Anthem for you.'

'Please don't. It's not my favourite song. Do you know YMCA?' Tom embraced him. 'When I saw you lying flat out, I thought you'd had a heart attack. And all our fault, working you to death. So a relief, you are OK.'

Tom said his goodbyes and left.

Lily was working on his cut. She had cleaned him up, and was wiping the gash with cotton wool and antiseptic.

'I couldn't get in the house,' she said. 'How was I to know the locks had been changed? I was ringing for a good fifteen minutes before Tom came down.'

It was too long a tale to fill her in on the story of why the locks had been changed, the threatening emails and Maggie's insistent on changing the front door locks. Too complicated this early. Someone else could tell her. He munched pizza so he wouldn't have to. He needed to talk to Maggie. She was the key.

Judy came in.

She was in running gear, shorts and T-shirt, and trainers. Her hair was tied back in a pony tail. Her forehead was sweaty. She was breathing heavily but recovering rapidly.

'Whatever happened to you, Jack?'

He was in the chair, Lily tending to him.

'I fell and knocked myself out,' he said, not wanting to give details of diabetic collapse. 'I'm fine.'

He was, more or less. Refuelled and feeling energised. Pity about the bandage which Lily was putting on. The mark of Cain. He had a cap at home, he'd wear that when he went back for his suit. Could he wear a cap in court, or was that disrespectful?

Jack could see her looking aghast at just the few cupboards on the wall, but what could she say with the builder being bandaged in the chair. She had obviously been out on her morning run. Amazing she could fit it in with her busyness.

'I'll work late tonight,' he said. 'I shall complete all the work.'

'I'll help.'

He was not sure he wanted her to, but thanked her.

The bandaging done, he stood up. Stretched his arms wide and swung them over his head with a clap. No broken bones, head a little sore, he was OK, even if he looked like the walking wounded.

'Thank you, Lily.' He embraced her.

'No problem, Jack.'

'Here's your keys,' he said, going to a drawer in the island and taking our a pair labelled Lily. He handed them over. 'Let me have your old ones when you are ready. Now I must go and see Maggie.'

He knew Judy had lots to say to him but didn't know how to say it to this combatant wounded in action. She wanted the kitchen done pronto and it had stalled. His plan had been to get another three cupboards on the wall before he left, with another three made up and ready. All jettisoned because he hadn't eaten.

So careless. Not that they were short of food here. Pizza galore and enough juice to float the Queen Mary.

'Back soon,' he said, not knowing how long he'd be.

He was going up the stairs, when there was Mo coming down, besuited and with a briefcase.

'Whatever happened to you, mate?'

'Fell over and hit my head. I'm fine. Just need a word with Maggie about security. Is she up?'

'She is. I'm the stop-in-bed. Must rush or I'll miss my train.'

And he was rushing down the stairs, rapidly out the front door, slamming it behind him.

Chapter 28

'Come in.'

Jack entered. Maggie was finishing making the bed. She put Paddington in place, on a pillow leaning against the headboard.

'It is silly,' she said, placing him exactly midway, 'and before you say anything, we don't sleep with him. Mo certainly wouldn't have that.' Satisfied with Paddington's enthronement, she turned to Jack. 'What have you done to your head?'

'I fell and banged it.' True with much omitted. 'But I'm fine. Lily bandaged me up.'

'Does it hurt?'

'A slight ache. Not much. Looks worse than it is with the bandage.'

'Can you work?'

'Yes,' he said with a certainty he wasn't sure of. 'I need to talk to you about the threatening emails.'

'We must have bolts on the back door,' she said. 'Like you said.'

He ignored her remark.

'I know who sent the emails,' he said.

'Mo's family? How do you know for sure?'

'You have to start with the smashed up kitchen. It all stems from that,' he said. 'I know who smashed it up, and it had nothing to do with Mo's family.'

'Who did it?'

'I can't tell you.'

'Why not?'

'I can't. Trust me. I know who did it, and Mo's family had no hand in it.'

'I wish you'd say.'

She was seated on the sofa, Jack had taken a chair. His head was throbbing, a metronome to his line of thought.

'The two threatening emails included the vandalised kitchen. The first said Second Warning, the second said Third Warning. That had to be the smashed kitchen as the first.'

She was nodding.

'So whoever sent them knew the kitchen had been damaged and was claiming it. There aren't many who knew, when the emails came in that the kitchen had been vandalised.' He enumerated on his fingers. 'That would be Judy, Tom, Mo, Lily, and Uncle Alec.'

'And me.'

'Let's leave you out. The first email came at half ten. At that time, Judy and Lily were with me cleaning up the kitchen. Neither of them had sent any emails, they were too busy bagging and sweeping. So that leaves Uncle Alec, Mo and Tom.'

'I am afraid what you are going to say,' she said, her fingers rapping on the arm of the sofa. 'Go on.'

'Uncle Alec couldn't have sent the first email, as he didn't know the kitchen was damaged then, finding out only when he came later and the first email had already been sent.'

'Leaving Tom or Mo,' she said. 'I can't believe it, my brother or my fiance. Awful whoever of them.'

'Tom likes to taunt people,' Jack went on. 'But only certain people. Never me or Judy. And he wouldn't have a go at you.'

She threw up her hands.

'Not Mo! Never my darling Mo. We are getting married tomorrow. He wouldn't dream of sending me such vile messages.'

'Are you sure?'

'Totally. One hundred percent. Never my darling Mo. He would not stoop to such a thing. We play music together. He comes with me to my gigs. We are getting married. Never Mo.'

'I agree. When he came home yesterday and found out you hadn't phoned him about the emails, he was distraught. That wasn't put on. Mo is no actor.'

She stared at him. 'But that leaves no one. We are back where we started.'

'No. There's one we haven't discussed.'

Her head fell into her hands. He waited. There were weaknesses in his reasoning, she could challenge him. Always the risk in a confrontation. Sometimes it paid off and other times, it didn't.

'I sent them,' she said quietly, lifting her head to face him. She smiled wryly. 'Are you going to the police?'

'I won't. If you give me the phone you used.'

He watched her, her face contorting, struggling with what he had told her and her admission. But she couldn't back out. Maybe to the cops but not to him.

Maggie put her hand under the other cushion of the sofa, dug deep and pulled out a tablet. She handed it to him.

'Whose is this?' he said.

'My father's. I found it under the wardrobe when we were getting rid of his furniture. The cops had missed it, but Cliff had confessed by then, so they weren't very thorough in their search.'

'What's on it?'

'Not much. I deleted the emails I sent. Though there is a file I can't open.'

That would be for later. Might be something, might be nothing at all.

'My turn,' she said.

'To do what?'

'To tell you what I know, Jack Bell, private investigator. I looked you up. I thought this builder is too curious, asking too many questions. Too interested in the murder of our father. Your web page gives you away. A photo even, of the builder and private investigator. A weird combination. Judy employed you obviously. All very sneaky, you working away, worming your way into our confidence. And then it came to me, it was obvious, who smashed up the kitchen.'

'Who do you think?'

'It had to be Judy,' she said. 'She wanted to employ you to find the killer and get her twin brother off. She needed you to work as a builder in the kitchen, to listen in to our chatter, talk to us, win us over. An undercover detective. But there was no work to do in the kitchen. The cupboards are only a couple of years old. The kitchen was in good repair. So she made some damage. Some work for you.'

He smiled. Maggie was sharp. 'You are fond of Judy.'

'I am. We argue, well what sisters don't, but we support each other. She gives me work at her events. And she's running the wedding, organising everything. Marquee, catering, music, photographer. She's my mate.'

'DS Taylor also worked out who smashed up the kitchen,' said Jack.

'Yes. She was all but accusing Judy. Another tale was necessary to take the heat off her. So I constructed one. You know how it goes. The new testament. Someone from Mo's family smashed the kitchen as a warning and was threatening to kill me if I married Mo.' She laughed. 'Best bit of acting I've done since college.'

'Well, it worked. DS Taylor has told me that the emails confuse the issue. She thought Judy or me had smashed the kitchen, but with the complication of the emails it would never get to trial. Were you going to send any more?'

She shrugged. 'No need. My scenario says Mo's family did it and they have been warned off.'

'You and Judy have certainly created work for the cops.'

'Could get us in big trouble. But you are not going to grass on us, are you, Jack?'

'Judy is employing me. And I like you.'

'Oh I'd marry you, if I hadn't met Mo.'

She was most definitely flirting. But so was he.

'Should I laugh or cry? At missing out.'

'Oh cry, Jack, at the wedding. I'll weep too.'

'There's still 24 hours.'

She waved a disparaging hand. 'No chance.'

'All the best ones are gone when you get to my age,' he said. 'Partnered, married or off men. But I won't grass, consider that a wedding present. Just keep it to yourself that I'm not just a builder.'

Though he couldn't quite get it out of his head that she might be the killer. She was smart enough and could act the innocent for Hollywood. He didn't want her to be, but her attraction didn't null her as a suspect.

'I shall keep mum,' she said. 'I haven't told Mo, about why you are really here or me sending the emails. I wanted to, having involved his family. Perhaps in ten years time when he's confessing a sin, I'll balance his with mine.' She laughed. 'But I am glad you know. It takes a weight off. And handing over that wretched tablet is no loss. Wipe my fingerprints off it. Or best of all, throw it in the Thames.'

Chapter 29

On his way back to the kitchen, he could hear Lily hoovering the sitting room. The noise was too much for his aching head. He hurried along to the kitchen, where Judy was assembling one of the flatpacks.

He must have been longer with Maggie than he realised, as Judy had obviously showered, and was now in T-shirt and jeans other than running gear.

'I think I've got the hang of these,' she said of the cupboard she was assembling. 'From the one you left half done.'

'Have you got any paracetamol?' he said.

She went to a drawer in the island.

'Is it bad?'

'It comes and goes.' He took two pills from her, and downed them with a glass of water.

'What's that tablet?' she said. He had laid it on the counter.

'Maggie gave it to me. Might be of interest.'

'You were a long time talking to her.'

'Security stuff,' he said, lying off the cuff. 'Bolts for the back door, a burglar alarm with motion sensors, checking the window locks. She is quite scared.'

'You were some time in her bedroom. Remember, she is getting married tomorrow.'

'Didn't touch her. Strictly business.'

She smiled as if she didn't quite believe him. No bad thing if she were a little jealous. He would have to tell her about her sister sending the emails, as she was employing him, but not just yet.

'What we going to do about the work here?' said Judy.

He looked about the kitchen, thinking how much had to be done to get it straight before the wedding rushing towards them like a tsunami.

'I'm going to have to leave now,' he said. 'To get to the court on time. Why don't you assemble the rest of the cupboards, and, after we have visited Cliff, we'll put them all up.'

'I suppose that's the best we can do,' she said reluctantly. 'You go and I hope you can help your daughter. I'll assemble the remaining cupboards, and be at your place at 2.15 to pick you up for our trip to Pentonville.'

He pecked her on the cheek. She grasped him and rounded it into a long kiss. A throbbing head muted the pleasure, but more was to come, the act told him, when he could give in to it.

When they broke, she held him for a few seconds by his hand, as if reluctant for him to go. But he had a tight timetable. A daughter at court.

'See you later,' he said, picking up the tablet and blowing her a kiss.

He left. Quick march, less he be drawn back. Lily was now hoovering the TV room, as he opened the front door and was out of the house.

Free in the warming summer air, so many entanglements in that house. Even as he climbed into his van, he felt the magnetism that might so easily draw him back.

He drove home.

Just as well Maggie was getting married. He would not transgress there. She was one smart lady. An actress, a singer songwriter, sharp and compelling. No wonder Mo counted himself lucky. She had sent the emails to herself from the tablet he now had. Her father's, found under the wardrobe. He must have put it there, not wanting anyone to know of it. Jack must have a good look at it.

If he could find time in his over full timetable.

Back home, he washed carefully, not wanting to shower with the bandage. He shaved and put on his only suit. He hated wearing it. It felt like a straitjacket, and was reserved for court appearances and funerals.

He had a bowl of Mia's muesli with some fruit juice, not having time to cook, resolving to eat regularly. His stupidity in the early morning rankled, though all in all, it had been an eventful few hours. A confession from Maggie and a kiss from Judy. And a diabetic coma. That could be deadly. He knew the rules well enough. Simple, so simple. Eat little and often. Not as if it was a problem in that kitchen. With a fridge full of food, close by.

What a dope.

Suit on, with dress shoes, and tie, one of three, what a palaver. He looked in the mirror in the bathroom. He was gazing at a con man, except for the bandage that revealed him as a prize fighter who had lost his last bout.

He put on his cap. Hardly any better. But it would have to do. And left the house with a small backpack containing nothing but a notebook and pen.

Chapter 30

Jack walked to Forest Gate station. He would go to Baker Street, a good destination for a private investigator, though he never felt quite honest giving himself that title, a sort of fraud. Maybe it would feel real after his 100th case.

Or if he cracked this one.

He bought a ticket. Jack didn't catch trains often. Most of his work was local and he drove to work and to pick up gear. The van was his tool store as well as his transport. On the platform, he was self-conscious in his suit, added to by the bandage, still visible under his cap.

The journey was simple enough. The Elizabeth line to Farringdon, then Metropolitan line to Baker Street. Half an hour on the train, and he'd given himself an hour.

The train was crowded. He had hit the rush hour, and had to stand for a few stops. At Stratford half the train got off and he took a seat and tried to relax. He hoped Judy would assemble the remaining cupboards. Then the work would get done, otherwise it was touch and go. Though she was so often on the phone to someone or other for the wedding or the various events she was organising, that whether she'd find time for the cupboards was yet to be seen. But she wanted them all up, having rather overdone the vandalism. An irony there.

Which all missed the point of it. The cupboards had become primary, but they were the excuse to have him working at the house, so he could find out who murdered Richard Ffrench. But it seemed the cupboards had taken over and pushed the case aside.

Deadlines. Time was rushing in on him like a mighty wave.

But his headache had gone. One good thing, though courts made him nervous. He had had a court case two years ago, with him in the dock. Short enough, but stressful. It was an assembly belt. Case after case, the magistrates and lawyers talking to each other, like it was their club, making it difficult for anyone else to know what was going on.

Take it as it comes. He may or may not be able to speak up for Mia. It was likely she was going to prison. Locking themselves to Downing Street; he couldn't see her and her mates getting away with a fine. He was unsure what he felt about it. It was good she was standing up for her principles, while most people, himself included, were apathetic, but would it do any good?

He hoped she wouldn't make a big fuss in court. Yelling, *Stop Climate Change, Fossil Fuels Out!* And adding months to her sentence. Worthy as such sentiments may be.

But one thing he was sure about, she wouldn't be going home with him. Once sentenced, she would go straight down to the holding cells, to await the van that would take her to prison.

Every offence from shoplifting to murder started at the magistrates court. The minor ones were dealt with there but the major ones were sent on to crown court, where there would be a jury trial. He hoped that Mia's case was held to be minor enough for the magistrates court to deal with. The maximum sentence there was six months, while at crown court the sky was the limit.

Jack had picked up some of this from his own experience and some from Nova, a detective sergeant, who he'd been with for two years. Until the break up. He'd hardly thought about her this morning. No bad thing. What with working, collapsing and the two Ffrench women. Sisters in crime.

Judy and Maggie's offences, if the truth came out, and they went to court, very likely it would be crown court. Wasting police time was treated very seriously. And he'd got himself involved, condoning Judy's offence, lying to the police about it. He had had the option to walk away but the money in the bank had seduced him.

Jack alighted at Farringdon and followed the signs for the Metropolitan line. Another crowded train, and no seat. Just a few stops though. Quite a few men in suits, smartly dressed women. The working class started earlier in the day. What would these be? Civil servants, lawyers and all sorts of professional people. Tom, though, had left early, with an imperative to come up with a world shattering slogan for a chocolate bar, in spite of his cynicism.

Could Tom have strangled his father? If he'd found out about the draft will, so close to getting signed, maybe. Though that could be said for Maggie, Judy and Cliff. Could he rule Mo out? He would do very well out of Maggie's inheritance once they were married, but not if her allotment had been cut as in the draft will.

The information from Nova on the draft will homed him in on the family. There were four of them. Would Judy have employed him if she was the killer? On top of which, Cliff had withdrawn his confession. How would that be dealt with in court? Was it still regarded or had it become scrap paper?

Not that withdrawing a confession was proof of innocence. It simply meant he was going to fight his case.

She wanted a result by tomorrow. Might as well draw a name from a hat.

Jack alighted at Baker Street. A confusing station, how do you get out of it? He followed the people, then the exit signs, until he was on the street. But what street? He brought up the map on his phone, and orientated himself with a named side street, started walking and checked with another. It fitted. He was on the Marylebone Road, and going in the right direction.

The road was chock-a-block with traffic on both sides, the fumes choking. Mia would point out such things, showing him that most of the cars had one person in. This was climate change in action, with the majority of the cars using fossil fuel.

And now she was in court, trying to get the government to make all these drivers come to work by train or bus or to buy an electric car. The latter not cheap. Better still, get a bike, like she had done.

His gas guzzler, though, he would use till it fell to bits. No choice in the matter. Could he afford then to go electric? Second hand perhaps. Or if the government offered drivers a deal to switch. The sort of thing he would chat to Mia about, but not for some time if she was banged up for six months or more.

Jack arrived at the Westminster Magistrates Court, a large modern building, that if you didn't know could have been a college. He looked at his watch, ten minutes early. He took a deep breath of polluted air and stepped inside.

Coming into a long, wide, and high hallway that echoed with the conversations of the many people along its length. Easy enough to tell the accused from the lawyers, both wore suits but the lawyers carried files, and didn't stare about them searching for a guardian angel.

Once through the metal detector, having no gun or knife, he was unsure where to go. He had googled Westminster Magistrates court at home, and found out there were ten courts. A lot of crime going on. He had no idea which one Mia was to appear in. There must be a list somewhere.

He wandered through the throng, deciding to walk down to the end, hoping to see her, if not he'd ask someone. The courts had wide doors, each numbered, he had passed 1, 2 and 3, each with an attendant in uniform standing by.

When he had come to court himself, not this one, but much the same, he had been brought in a black maria in handcuffs, and kept in a holding cell until he was led into court, accused of murder. He was hardly five minutes in court as his case was passed along to crown court. It was unlikely Mia was in a holding cell, though he couldn't be sure as she had been held overnight.

It was an uncomfortable walk down the corridor, reminding him of his time in court. How many of these people wouldn't be going home after their case?

Then he saw her, in a throng, outside court 5. She saw him, and called, 'Dad!' and rushed over. They embraced.

'What did you do to your head?' she said.

'Fell over and bashed it.'

'Were you sober?'

'Totally. Just clumsy.'

Her chestnut hair was somewhat untidy, long and straggly. She wore a red T-shirt with black lettering saying *Climate Emergency*, blue jeans and trainers. If he'd have thought about it, he might have brought her a less strident T-shirt, but she probably would have scorned it.

She led him to a small group. Two young women and a young man. The two young women were casually dressed like Mia. He guessed they were her co-accused. The young man wore a suit and had a bundle of files under his arm. He looked too young but must be their lawyer.

'This is my dad,' she said, 'he's a builder and a private eye.'

'I am just your dad this morning,' said Jack. And went around shaking hands, introducing himself.

'Are you their solicitor?' he said to the young man, who had introduced himself as Gareth.

'I am,' he said with a friendly smile.

'Can we have a word?' Jack drew him aside, away from the three women. 'What's likely to happen?' he said.

'Well, they are guilty. There is no doubt of that. Not in my eyes, but in the eyes of the law. I am working pro bono, as a supporter of climate activists. I am hoping the case won't get passed onto crown court. If it is dealt with here the maximum sentence is six months, if it goes to crown court and a jury trial, they could get two years.'

'Two years!' exclaimed Jack. That was serious time in a seventeen year old's life.

'Or longer. Crown court deals harshly there with climate protesters. It's a scandal really, the judges mostly ultra respectable old men out to make examples of youth. As if climate change won't affect them and their families. Your daughter tells me she wants to go to crown court and have a trial by jury, as is her right. I have tried to persuade her that she is much better off being dealt with here, but she has this romantic idea that a jury couldn't possibly find her guilty.'

Jack nodded. That was his daughter all over. He noticed that three others had joined the other women defendants. One looked like a mother, another a father, the other either a relative or friend.

'I'll talk to her,' he said.

He went over to the group, said hello to the newcomers and drew his daughter aside.

'You are thinking of going to crown court,' he said.

'Yes. Trial by jury, rather than these old fogy magistrates.'

'You could get two years or more,' he said.

'I could get off. I just need to persuade the jury that I am fighting on their behalf.'

'Who says you'll be allowed to? Old fogies make the rules there, what you can say and can't say. It's two years you have to think about. In some stinking jail, ordered about by screws, lousy food, and banged up in a cell most of the day. How's that going to stop climate change?'

'The jury might free me.'

'I bet they won't.'

'You don't know.'

'Neither do you. But I have been to prison, and I tell you, I never want to go back again. Full of petty rules, drugs, the mentally ill, and dangerous people. They'll eat you alive.'

'But if I am freed, having convinced the jury that climate change is the biggest catastrophe facing the planet, then what would you say?'

'I'd say you are a dreamer. The world isn't so good. The jury will be told that they must find you guilty as you were caught in the act.'

'That was the whole point. We wanted to be caught, so we could make our case.'

'Where's the press? Where's the TV cameras?'

'Oh, you are such a downer. Just one of the oldies, your mind fixed.'

'And who do you think will be on the jury? College students?'

'You are so depressing, Dad.' She folded her arms stubbornly.

'I don't want you spending two years in jail, Mia.'

She didn't reply, had his arguments sunk in or was she stuck in her obstinate quicksand?

'Please don't opt for crown court,' he said. 'You need to march and make banners. Give speeches. Not be banged up in a smelly cell.'

She grimaced, whether at him or the thought of two years in a smelly cell, he couldn't say.

'All right,' she finally said. 'I'll take what comes here. Six months max, I can handle that.'

Chapter 31

They waited some time before going into court. Jack spotted a sheet on the wall by the court door, saying which cases would be held in the court that day. They were third on the list.

Once Mia had decided that she would take her punishment here, she was fervent in persuading her colleagues that magistrates court was best for them.

'Well done,' said the young lawyer to Jack.

'I've been to prison,' he said. 'Wrongly accused. I had some good people on the outside who got me out.'

One of whom was Mia. Now it had been his turn to save her from a long sentence. Another was Nova, who he had hardly thought about this morning. And his ex, Alison. Two exes who fought for him.

A lesson there; don't burn your bridges.

Jack spoke to the mother of one of the women, who was quite depressed that her daughter was going to prison. Someone has to fight, he told her. Gandhi went to prison, Nelson Mandela, and the suffragettes. Martin Luther King went to jail many times on trumped up charges, and for civil disobedience. He was quoting Mia, an essay she had written.

'Don't you mind?' said the woman.

'I'm glad she's not taking drugs. Or obsessed with slimming. Maybe we should be marching. Who else is going to change the world?'

He was convincing himself if not her, but she did seem a little cheerier.

'Could be worse,' she admitted.

At last they got into court. Three magistrates were raised high on throne-like chairs, under a picture of King Charles. There were pews of light wood, possibly oak, he thought. And a central table for the clerk, lawyers and press, but there were no press. The young women were yesterday's news.

The three women crowded into the witness stand. They had been told to be respectful by Gareth. No chanting or name calling. It would only get them a longer sentence, for no gain.

The charge was read out by the clerk, gluing themselves to the railings at the top of Downing Street. The three women answered to the their names. Gareth introduced himself as their solicitor.

The policeman was called for. The one on duty at the gates of Downing Street. There was no response. The clerk and magistrates got into a hushed huddle. Jack perked up; a key witness not here.

'Where is he?' asked the chief magistrate.

Jack managed to hear the clerk mumble, 'Operational duties.'

'Do we need the policeman?' said the chief magistrate.

'Yes sir,' said Gareth, standing up and facing the bench, eager to be part of the process. 'The defence has a right to hear from the main witness for the crown. Who is also the arresting officer. In dual capacity, the defence must be able to question him.'

A firebrand. Jack was impressed.

'Shouldn't this go to crown court?' the head magistrate asked the clerk.

Jack was alarmed. Oh no.

Gareth was out of his seat.

'No one was hurt, sir. No traffic hold up, no resisting arrest.'

'But it was Downing Street, the offices of the Prime Minister.'

'It was simply to make a point,' said Gareth. 'No harm was done to anyone. They are just young women. I am sure they will never do this again.'

'But it was Downing Street,' repeated the Chief Magistrate.

'Might I say something, your honour,' said Mia from the witness stand.

'Go on, young lady.'

'It was a thoughtless act,' she said. 'Our intention was not to hurt anyone, but just get some publicity for climate change, so parliament might act. We are deeply sorry.'

'I sympathise with your cause, young lady. But you chose Downing Street. A very thoughtless act.'

'We'd like to be judged in this court,' she said. 'If your honours so please. And not waste the time of crown court, which has much more serious cases to deal with, your honours.'

Was she overdoing 'your honours'? Which Jack knew was reserved for judges, not magistrates, but maybe it did no harm to butter them up.

The three magistrates went into conclave. Jack wondered how sorry Mia was, knowing his impetuous daughter.

The magistrates whispered to the clerk. The clerk was the expert in law, the magistrates were lay people. Back and forth went their chat, unheard by the court. The chief magistrate nodded. Something had been decided.

'This case is postponed,' he said. 'It will be held in this court. Postponed until next Friday. Please make sure the arresting officer attends. Next case.'

They left the court, the girls jubilant, as if they had won.

Chapter 32

Jack and Mia went round the corner to Marylebone station on Mia's suggestion. There, they had a coffee and a cake in one of the coffee shops. Mia was over the moon, as if she had won the lottery.

'I thought I was off to jail,' she said, 'but I am out and free. Look at me, people! The fuzz didn't get me.'

Free for a week, thought Jack. But he didn't want to dent her exuberance. He was pleased too. He had persuaded Mia to accept punishment at the magistrates court, rather than go for a jury trial at crown court with a more hefty penalty. And little chance of getting off.

A six month's sentence seemed a long time, but then stacked against a two year one, not so long.

'Nice little speech from the box,' he said. 'I think it swayed them.'

'Gareth says so too. But you are right, Dad. Crown court could have massacred us.'

'Do you want me to come next Friday?'

'Yes, please, but it's pretty obvious I won't be coming home. It was touch and go back there; they were thinking of sending us to crown court. Good job we were able to change their mind. I hope we get the same magistrate next week. Max of six months, could get it, the way they were talking. But if we do, then you get half off for good behaviour, so it's three really as I don't intend hitting a guard or starting a fire. Should be out by the end of October. Won't miss much school; term finishes in a week for the summer, doesn't start again until September. So that's half of it. I wonder if I could study there.'

'Your mum could talk to your teachers about giving you school work.'

'No moon or stars in the nick,' she said. 'As soon as I'm out we go over the Flats with the scope.'

'Of course we will.'

They set off home. Once there, he got out of his suit. He hadn't needed it, but you never knew. He'd felt shackled in it, though next week he'd have to endure it again, but the bandage would be off.

He had been of use, persuading Mia to go for the lower court. So not a waste of time. But same again next week.

Mia took a bath to get rid of the prison smell. She had some of her clothes at her father's, most at her mother's, but enough here.

Eat. Little and often.

Jack had a cheese sandwich and an apple. More fruit and veg was the other half of the prescription, but who's perfect? But he admitted, he could get a little closer to the doctor's instruction. It wasn't good collapsing, being in a coma for a good hour. Not good at all.

He could be dead. Little and often. Repeat.

Jack made a cup of tea, and while drinking it had a look at the electronic tablet Maggie had given him. A few years old, not the latest. Maggie had told him that she had cleaned off the threatening emails. There was no sign of them, nor any others in the email program. The usual apps, but he was looking for files.

He found one, just one, but it was password protected. That was meaningful. This was Richard Ffrench's machine. He tried Ffrenchco. Too obvious.

Mia came out of the bathroom.

'Any good at cracking passwords?' he said.

She came over.

'That's an old machine,' she said. 'Not much RAM, slow downloads.'

'Can you get into that file?'

'I can't, but I know someone who might be able to. When do you want it for?'

'Soon as possible. It's for the job I'm working on. Could be important. It belonged to a murdered man.'

The doorbell rang.

'That's for me. I'm off on a prison visit. Then I have to work, have to get that kitchen done today. Must keep the customer happy.'

'Client,' she corrected him.

'The people who pay me. Got to make a living. Don't know when I'll be back. Just late.'

He said his goodbyes and was off out.

At the door was Judy with a taxi.

'Quick, Jack. Let's get on the move. Mustn't be late.'

He followed her to the black cab. They got in, seat belts on and the cab set off.

'How did it go at court?' she asked.

'Postponed,' he said. 'The arresting cop didn't show up. Back again next week. And cross fingers for a half decent outcome.'

He kept it simple with no wish to go into the details of crown court versus magistrates court. And how he'd persuaded Mia to go for the latter. A relief, the postponement, and on to the next hurdle where she was bound to fall.

They were sitting side by side. She had a little sawdust on her jeans.

'How did you get on with the cupboards?' he said.

'I assembled four. I was getting good at it. Kept getting interrupted by phone calls.'

She took his hand. He imagined a life with Judy would keep getting interrupted by phone calls.

He laughed, thinking of another woman who got inconvenient phone calls.

'What is so funny?'

'I'm thinking of Nova. You know DS Taylor. We were together two years.'

'I thought there was something going between you two.'

'Our life was broken up by phone calls. It could be in a restaurant, the cinema, once out on Wanstead Flats, with my telescope, we had coffee and pizza, all set for an evening of stargazing. The phone rang and she left me with the moon and the Plough. Another murder. We argued over it. She dumped me, I dumped her. Only this time, it's final, she has someone else. To annoy with urgent calls.'

'Does that damn our relationship before it's even started?'

He noted she said 'relationship' as if she were contemplating such a thing. Some movement perhaps.

'We can but try,' he said, hope springing eternal. 'Tell me something. The marriage tomorrow. Maggie has so much more money than Mo. How will that work out?'

'They have a prenup.'

'What's that when it's in long trousers?'

'A prenuptial agreement. You must have heard of it. When one party is a lot richer than the other.'

'I've never heard of it. I obviously mix in the wrong circles.'

'British divorce law divides everything up 50/50. That's if there are no children involved and it's a long marriage. A prenup prevents that. In the case of a divorce Mo would get some but nowhere near half. Just what's allowed him in the prenup. I helped write it.'

'It rather takes the romance out,' he said, 'preparing for a divorce when you are getting married.'

'Realism,' she said. 'Around 40 per cent of marriages end in divorce in this country. They start off starry-eyed, thinking their marriage is eternal, and end up cursing each other. You were married to Mia's mother?' He nodded. 'How did that end up?'

'Disastrously. She kicked me out. I was drinking like a fish. I was on the streets for two weeks. I hardly remember it. Then a few months in a Salvation Army hostel, managed to stop drinking more or less, and began piecing my life together. Did a carpentry class for three months and bluffed my way into a building job.' He laughed. 'And here we are. My path to success.'

'I was married,' she said, with a shrug. 'We broke up after two years. I suspect the phone calls were a factor, his as well as mine. He is a manager for a number of bands. It was an amicable split. There had been no prenup. No court battle. We'd simply lost interest in each other. No excitement. Sad really. I see him sometimes at events. He's married, two kids. We have the odd drink together, compare notes.'

They were going through the City. Traffic congested, busy pavements, easier to walk except for the pollution held in the valley by the banks and other financial buildings. Drivers weren't immune, they got it too, breathing in the fumes from the tailpipe in front.

Making him think of Mia. A postponement, that was all. The law would get her sure enough. He hoped her prison wasn't too far away, so he could visit without a day's travel.

Judy interrupted his thoughts.

'That long conversation you had with Maggie this morning...' she said.

Time to come clean. She was paying him. Half up front. Beyond the sham building work, he hadn't given her much. This, at least, was worth paying for.

'I worked out she was sending the threatening emails,' he said.

Judy was agape. 'She, my sister. To herself!'

'Hard to believe,' he said. 'But once I'd eliminated everyone else, it had to be Maggie. I confronted her with it, and she admitted it.'

'Wow, that's some revelation. Why would she do that?'

'She worked out that you broke up the kitchen. Maggie is sharp. And she saw that Nova, the cop, had got that far too. So she thought she'd confuse matters.'

'Still not sure I get it.'

'Making the cops think it was all of a piece. Smashing of the kitchen, followed by the threats. Same person. So you

158

wouldn't be seen as the vandal smashing the kitchen. Bringing in Mo's family to muddy the water.'

'Got it. Cunning plan. Maggie is such a convincing liar. She did music and drama at college, but, even so, such bare-faced effrontery. She was going on and on about how it was Mo's family out to kill her. The cops went round there to warn them off. One dropped in this morning to make sure everything was OK. They'll be at the wedding in case the troll shows up with a shotgun.' She turned to him. 'And it's all made up.'

'Started by you,' he couldn't help saying.

'I can't say I am not grateful to Maggie, but I was so sure it was Mo's family. Even Mo thought so. She won't be sending any more, will she?'

'No.'

He didn't say anything about the tablet he had taken from Maggie. With the password protected file. Could Mia get it opened via one of her nerd pals? If not, he could take the tablet to Nova and get the cops to break into the file. But there were added complications to that. Although, Maggie had deleted her emails, Nova had told him that their computer experts could often find deleted information on phones and computers. And if they found the emails, he'd be faced with awkward questions. Like who gave him the tablet.

They had been silent for a few minutes. Companionable. He contemplating the password protected file and its implications, while Judy was getting to grips with the fact that Maggie had sent the death threats to herself. Perhaps thinking of the consequences if that were found out. For both sisters.

They arrived at Pentonville.

Chapter 33

Jack and Judy went through the rigmarole necessary for prison visits, at the visitors centre, at the front of the prison. Separated from the prison, the centre attempted to be friendlier than the prison itself with its metal doors, long corridors and the barnyard smell. This was the interface between the outside world and the prison; visitors could get tea and a bite to eat. Judy knew the drill, being a regular visitor. The checks, the forms to be signed, both were given wrist bands.

Cliff was on remand, as he hadn't had his trial yet, and so was allowed more visits. Judy left some art materials at the desk that Cliff had requested. They had to be checked that they were free of drugs or other contraband before being handed on to Cliff. Could be a couple of days. Nothing could be taken into the visitors hall beyond themselves. There was a row of lockers, like at a swimming pool. Jack and Judy took one, she put in her handbag, and both their phones, and locked it, before being escorted to the visiting hall.

The hall was busy. Convicted prisoners were only allowed one visit a month, but with over 1000 prisoners in Pentonville, that was a lot to fit in each month, and then there were the remand prisoners, like Cliff, allowed three visits a week.

There were about 20 tables with prisoners and visitors at each. Convicted prisoners were easy to spot, most wore prison garb, baggy tracksuit type gear. Remand prisoners could wear their own clothes. The room was noisy with chatter, there were children here and there, a girl on a mother's lap sucking a lollipop, a boy playing with farm animals on the floor. How had he smuggled them in? But the prison guards, four of them seated around the room, ignored the infringement, appearing somewhat bored. There were more women visitors than men, not surprising as this was a men's prison.

Cliff was at a table on his own awaiting them. Being on remand, he wore his own clothes, a green T-shirt and jeans. Cliff rose to greet them. He had a black eye and a large plaster on his chin.

Judy hugged her brother. This was allowed at beginning and end of a visit. Jack shook his hand. He was very like Judy, the same light brown hair and snub nose. Though he'd obviously been in the wars. She was slimmer with all her running, while her twin brother was putting on weight with stodgy prison food.

'How did that happen,' she said when all were seated, looking at the injuries to his face.

'I looked at a guy,' said Cliff. 'He had an interesting face, weather worn, though more likely drugs worn. Beautiful people don't interest me, all the character smoothed out of their faces, but his was lived in, like a blues singer. But he didn't like me staring. Him and a mate came over and beat me up.'

'This is a jungle,' said Judy.

'But they messed up,' said Cliff. 'I've been drawing some portraits, and this don, name of Little, saw one of them, and wanted me to draw him. Little is the size of an elephant, irony, prison nicknames. So I drew him. I can do ten minute portraits, good likenesses. Made some money doing it at Forest Gate Festival last year. Just with charcoal, the basic sketch prettied up with pastels. Little loved it. So I did his mate, Large, half his size. Little and Large run drugs and phones. When they heard what happened to me, they sorted the two guys out. They're in the infirmary.'

'Won't they be after you when they come out?' said Judy.

'No. They know what they'll get. And so does everyone else. Did you get me those art supplies, sis?'

'Yes,' said Judy. 'They are being checked over.'

'Everyone wants their portrait now. Not always easy. You can't just wander about how you like. It has to be arranged with the screws. Though I managed a couple in the gym. I don't charge. Little says I should, fags or dope, but I reckon it's better to make friends. I've done about ten, and there's quite a few more I haven't got round to. And it gave me an idea. I want to do sketches of prison life. You know, the gym, the library, visiting hall, the kitchen, exercise yard, even the screws, in fact I've done a couple of pictures of them. It pays to keep in.'

'You are making Pentonville sound like a holiday camp,' said Judy.

'It's not. Food is terrible, and there are dangerous people here. But you have to find ways to survive or you'll hang yourself. And I have a skill. The art tutor came to see me, he wants me to help out at his classes. So could be a lot worse. I'm off drugs, the Ville did that for me. And I haven't got the hassle of Dad belittling me. I'm OK. I've asked to see the governor about doing the prison pictures, maybe getting them published as a book.'

'Sounds like you don't want us to get you out.'

'Don't get me wrong, sis, I want out. I want to see the sky, I want to walk on the Flats. I'm just making life bearable by keeping busy, by making friends.'

A prison guard yelled, 'Time!'

People started rising and hugging.

'Not us,' said Cliff. 'That's just the cons. They started half an hour before us. Remand prisoners are on a different timetable.'

In a few minutes, three quarters of the hall had gone. The prisoners remaining were less identifiable, wearing everyday clothing. Over half the tables were empty. It was quieter, a little more relaxed. There were still a few children though the boy with the farm animals had gone. A guard came round with a tray of tea for the guards on duty.

'You retracted your confession,' said Jack. It was the first words he'd said to Cliff beyond his initial greeting.

'It's all part of the same thing,' he said. 'I'm waking up. Judy here got me a psychiatrist, Dot. I've been seeing her once a week and she is good.'

'Not cheap,' said Judy to Jack. 'One hundred fifty pounds for a one hour session. Travelling time, she says.'

'Worth it and more,' said Cliff.

'I don't begrudge it.'

'I was doing lots of drugs before I came here,' said Cliff. 'Heroin, weed, snow. And I was having hallucinations. Seeing things, imagining I was doing things. It got to the point that I didn't know whether I had done some things or not. Dot went through it with me, over and over. I certainly wanted to kill Dad, just to get him off my back, his constant griping, telling me to get a proper job, and that he wasn't going to keep subsidising me much longer. It wears you down, the disparaging. And when he was murdered, I was sure I had done it. I had imagined it so often, I could see myself doing it, he in bed asleep, me slipping the cord round his neck and pulling it tight until he stopped breathing. And doing a dance of joy.'

'Did you have no doubt?' asked Jack.

'Some. But I figured if it wasn't me then it would have to be Judy, Tom or Maggie. And with my life at rock bottom, what the hell did it matter where I spent it. I was still in a state, drugs and all, so pretty sure, I did it. I strangled him as he slept, I told the cops, and gave them my confession. Dot turned that over. Made me see I was hallucinating. Though there is a chance I did it. I just can't be sure, I was so out of it. But I am claiming I didn't do it. When I stand up in court that's what I'll say. I won't tell them I have some doubt. So I have withdrawn my confession. My lawyers are on to it. Dot will be an expert witness on my behalf and we'll fight it out. In the meantime, I am going to be drawing to stay alive.'

Chapter 34

They left Pentonville and got a taxi back. Judy was relieved her brother wasn't crushed by prison, in fact was making the best of it with his drawings of prisoners, and the place itself. Jack was contemplating the withdrawn confession. Cliff was saying that his confession had been based on a drug-fuelled hallucination. He hadn't killed his father. But that was just for public consumption. In reality, he didn't know whether he had done it or not.

Cliff was still a suspect.

Back at the house, they went straight to the kitchen. Four cupboards were up on the wall, another six assembled waiting to be put up. And there, out of the window, he saw the marquee, taking up much of the lawn. He and Judy went out to inspect. The side facing the house was up for ease of access, the others down. Inside, four rows of trestle tables had been laid out. At the head of each row was a stack of chairs. There was a small row of trestle tables at the front, for the family, he assumed.

'You have to imagine them with tablecloths and flowers,' she said. 'We wanted to invite you to the dinner, me and Maggie, but felt we couldn't. There are only 80 guests; we had to turn down quite a few, and felt we couldn't sneak you in. Please come to the reception afterwards.'

Jack didn't mind at all not being invited to the dinner. If he had been, he'd be at one of the long trestle tables, not knowing anyone, and stuck in a suit. A good meal and boredom. And everyone asking, how did you do that to your head.

There were eight portable toilets along the fence. 80 guests, they'd certainly be needed, along with the house toilets.

As they were going back in, Jack saw the scrap wood from the broken-up cupboards was still on the patio.

'That was supposed to be picked up this afternoon,' he said.

'It can't stay,' said Judy. 'It's an eyesore.'

'Let's see what's happening.'

Jack dialled the chipboard factory. And was told that they had come an hour ago, and no one was in. The earliest they could come again was Monday.

Maggie came into the kitchen.

'Been swimming,' she said. 'It relaxes me. What with all that's going on. What's up?'

The reason why there was no one in.

'No one told me,' said Maggie. 'I was here for the marquee and the toilets. I didn't know about the scrap wood.'

'It's my fault,' said Judy. 'But the wood has to go. The patio is going to be a chill out zone.'

'I know a guy with a van,' said Jack. 'I'll give him a call.'

He dialled.

'Paul,' he said, once he was through. 'Can you take some scrap wood to Barking for me? Right away.'

'I'm busy, man. Rehearsing.'

Paul was a man with a van and a musician, getting by mostly. Jack held the phone away and mouthed to Judy: 'He's busy. How much can I offer.'

'Try two hundred.'

Jack gasped. All that for less than an hour's work. Well, she was paying.

'Two hundred quid, if you get here in fifteen minutes,' said Jack.

'Be there,' said Paul.

Call done, they got to work. Or at least Maggie and Judy did, assembling cupboards. Jack took some paracetamol; his head throbbing. He wondered whether it was the sight of the cupboards that set him off. The curse of them. Pointless work, to get the kitchen back to where it was.

He must push on. And found he could manage, if he kept it steady, no rushing. He had put up a cupboard when Paul arrived.

A middle aged hippy-cum-odd job man, grey hair to his shoulders, and in a great hurry.

'The band are so pissed off with me,' he said. 'But I can't turn down two hundred.'

Judy said, 'Another fifty if you take the rubbish away too. Just broken china. To the tip.'

'Load it up.'

The four of them loaded his van. Judy paid the money into his account as they worked. Jack gave him the address for the scrap wood.

'You at the festival tomorrow, Jack?' asked Paul.

'I'll be there. Mia's got a stall with her eco-mates.'

'We're playing at three thirty on the stage. Don't miss us. That's what the rehearsal is all about. I have to get a move on, be there and back, before they send out a hit man.'

And he was off.

Jack went back to putting cupboards up. All those yet to go up were assembled. Six on one side were on the wall, with six on the other side ready and waiting. They had a snack, and while eating decided they would all work at getting the cupboards up. Jack had his T-support, so could manage on his own, Maggie and Judy would work together.

They watched Jack putting up the first on the other side. Judy got the hang of it quickly. She had an eye for it and was handy with tools, working at events. Maggie would do what she was told.

In an hour, they had them all up.

'Let's get the doors on,' he said.

That was straightforward, all the hinges and screws in little packs. When they were all on, Jack had a sit down, whacked out.

'You OK, Jack?' inquired Maggie.

'Feeling a bit weak. Need a break.'

'Sit outside,' she said. 'We'll fill the cupboards.'

He took a chair on the patio, his view obscured by the marquee. The weakness, he knew had nothing to do with diabetes but all to do with the bang on the head. Any other time, he'd have taken the day off, but this work had to be done. He was grateful to have Maggie and Judy giving a hand.

Judy came out with a cup of tea and a cheese sandwich.

'You feeling any better, Jack?'

'Bit weak, but I can handle it. Let me eat this, and I'll be in with you.'

'You be the foreman,' she said. 'Tell us what to do and we'll get on with it.'

And that's how the kitchen cupboards and shelves were done. Once the cupboards were filled, the next job was the shelving. He showed them the fittings, and Judy got it at once. Seeing he wasn't needed, Jack did colour matching for the plaster patches on the wall, he'd filled in yesterday. A little black paint in the white he had, should work. He made up four test pots, a small amount for testing, with differing amounts of black well mixed in. All quite mathematical using cups and spoons, so he knew the proportions of black to white, and could scale up when he found the right match.

He painted the test strips on scrap cardboard. And borrowed a hair dryer for rapid drying. And then held the strips against the kitchen wall. None were perfect, one not too far off. Jack increased the black slightly in that pot. Painted the strip, and dried it.

More or less OK.

You could never quite tell with colour matching. It might be OK tomorrow, but in a few days the patches might stand out. But then, he wouldn't be here. Besides, it was tomorrow they were on show. What happened after that could be dealt with without panic.

Once the shelves were up, they sandpapered the bits of wall that he'd plastered yesterday, getting them smooth and flush. Jack did some, but his head was throbbing. He took some paracetamol, and rested up watching the two women at work. One a bride, pregnant, singing as she worked.

Once the sanding was done, there was the painting. In foreman mode, he told them to do it smoothly, so there wouldn't be brush marks. He crossed fingers it worked long term.

And with that, the kitchen was done. What a palaver to get back to where they were three days ago. All so he could be here to solve a murder. But all he'd been doing, it seemed, was taking down wrecked cupboards and replacing them with new.

They cleared up. Jack put his tools in the van, along with the fittings from the old cupboards, now gone to chipboard.

He said, 'I must go home. And rest up.'

Judy looked disappointed or was that his imagination?

'See you tomorrow,' she said, and gave a peck on the cheek.

He wished Maggie well for tomorrow. She thanked him for all the work he'd put in. And told him to come for the reception after the meal.

Jack got home, a little past eight o'clock.

Chapter 35

Jack all but collapsed on the sofa, holding his forehead.

'You OK?' said Mia.

She was working at the table, trying to get as much schoolwork done as possible before her impending prison sentence. She closed her laptop.

'My head,' he said. 'Dreadful headache.'

'You should go to hospital. Get an X-ray.'

'It'll pass,' he said. 'Just a bad headache.'

'No. You've had a knock. Come on, Dad, let's go. A girl on one of our demos got hit on the head with a police baton. She suffered it, didn't go to hospital and was dead two days later.'

'OK, I'll go. But before I forget. Take this lot.'

He gave her the bag of fittings.

Mia looked at them thoughtfully. 'Might be able to sell them tomorrow at the festival. But let's see to you.'

Jack allowed her to lead him out of the flat, agreeing it was sensible to check, if he didn't want to wake up dead. They got in his van and headed off to Newham hospital.

He had to concentrate as he drove, his head throbbing. Take it steady. Was it more than a headache?

Mia said, 'My mate opened that file. He has a program with every date in the last 100 years in numbers. People often use their birthdays as passwords. His program has more than 36 thousand dates. It tries them all out, takes about 10 minutes. And he got it. Lucky, as it could have been anything else, the name of a cat, where he was born. But it worked.'

Jack was driving steadily, half taking in what she had said, probably shouldn't be on the road, but it would have taken ages to get an ambulance and it was less than a ten minute drive. He pulled up by the side of the road.

'I can't concentrate and drive,' he said. 'What was in the file?'

'It was a prenup.'

'My God,' he said. 'Never heard of the word yesterday, then two come at once. Who was it between?'

'Hang about, I took a photo of the first page.' She clicked through her phone. 'Here it is. Between Richard Ffrench. Two fs. And Lily Brown.'

'That's the housekeeper. Well, well. When is it dated?'

'July 19th 2019.'

'Six years ago. Married.' He whistled. 'Certainly kept that secret. What does it say?'

'It's full of that awful language only lawyers can understand.'

'Keeps them in work. We have to employ them to explain it to us.'

'I had to go through it several times,' she said. 'But as far as I can make out, Lily in case of divorce gets nothing. While married, she has a flat and 5% of shares in his business. But divorced, zero.'

He thought about it, between the throbs in his head.

'Doesn't make sense,' he said. 'In the prenup, she gets nothing on divorce, and yet in his draft will, she gets the giant share. Why so generous?'

'Maybe he was going to divorce her,' said Mia.

'Then why give her the controlling share in the business in the draft will? Doesn't square. Got to think this out, when my head stops banging. If I'm not dead.'

They were several hours at the hospital. Having checked in, they sat in the waiting hall with around fifty others. Some with obvious ailments, others looking worried, perhaps with not much, the worried well or with something serious that wasn't obvious.

After an hour, Jack was given triage, a short assessment. Then things speeded up. He was sent for an X-ray. Following it, they waited for the results, Mia got them coffees, while he tried to work out how the prenup and the draft will meshed. And not getting anywhere.

A doctor called him in. Mia had accompanied him throughout. The doctor explained the X-ray, telling him that there was no internal bleeding or damage to the skull. As far as she could tell, he was OK. His fall was the reason for the headaches but should go in a day or so. If not, come back.

A nurse changed his dressing. It had become grubby with work. Jack was given a prescription for pain killers and sleeping pills. He handed them in at the hospital pharmacy. And after collecting the items, they left the hospital.

Back home, Jack had a bite to eat and dosed himself on the hospital medication. He was not aware of falling asleep.

It was past ten in the morning, when he woke up. He was lying on the sofa in his clothes, a duvet over him. On the table was a short note in Mia's handwriting:

Gone to set up for the festival. Come along.

Chapter 36

Half awake, he went into the kitchen. On the table was a bowl of muesli with sliced peaches on top, by it a jug of oat milk, and a small plate with a beigel of cheese and tomato. He must get a headache more often to get this treatment. He was touched; she wasn't just a nutty eco-warrior. Mia must have been out shopping. A pleasant surprise to start the day.

Jack made some tea, and settled down to a late breakfast. No headache this morning, and he'd slept like a baby. Building work was done at the house, so no rush, but the detective work yet to be completed. Though he had an inkling.

While eating, he wrote on a notepad: Uncle Alec, Lily, Cliff, Judy, Maggie, Mo, Tom. All with motives to murder Richard Ffrench. All with the opportunity. Cliff in jail for it, but he had withdrawn the confession that put him there. Would they still use it against him?

Jack might have stayed the night with Judy. It seemed that was the direction of travel. But his headache was a roadblock. That's the way of things. They hadn't had a fight, so who knows.

He wasn't thinking of Nova, until now. And that was more than a roadblock. An earthquake, the relationship smashed to rubble. We can be friends, she had said. True, but the words still stung.

His phone rang. It was his ex, Alison, Mia's mother.

'Hello, Alison.'

'Good morning, Jack. I hope your head is OK.'

She'd obviously spoken to Mia. Of course she had, wanting to know whether her daughter was in jail or not.

'Slept well, feel fine.'

'I'm glad of that. Mia told me the case had been postponed for a week.'

'Yes. I persuaded her that the magistrates court was best for her. The sentence there is limited to six months. Though it was touch and go. The magistrates were thinking of sending them to crown court. But Mia spoke up for them. Very polite, and she swung it.'

'Is she really going to jail?'

'Her lawyer thinks so. And picking Downing Street for a demo. Well, that is asking for trouble.'

'True.' A long sigh. 'It was going to happen sooner or later. She's been lucky so far. But she picked a dead cert loser this time round.'

'To get publicity. Though less than they hoped for. No journalists at the court.'

'I agree with her that climate change is on the march. That it has to be halted, Jack. But is breaking the law the way to change things?'

Jack could have given her Mia's reply. The suffragettes, Martin Luther King, Gandhi, all jailed at one time or another. Instead, he said:

'Ask me in 50 years.'

Alison laughed. 'We'll be dead or wish we were. Maybe drowned or baked to a crisp. Back to today. Our criminal daughter has a week of freedom. She's at her stall at Forest Gate Festival. I'm going. What about you?'

'In an hour or so.'

'Might see you then.'

She rang off. Quite a pleasant chat, all considered. She wasn't blaming him for their daughter's errant behaviour. As she had in past years. Mia was eighteen with a strong sense of morality but it didn't necessarily side with the law. Sometimes you have to break it, she had told him too many times. Or why live?

Too big a question. You must do something, Mia insisted. Or what is the point of being alive?

He hoped this was the peak for Mia. That she would hate jail and not want to go back again. Or the sentences would get longer.

Breakfast done with, he washed the dishes. Not many, just a few plates, nothing cooked. He was still wearing his working clothes, having slept in them. He sorted out clean clothes and had a bath. Easier to keep his bandage dry then under a shower. And enjoy the soak.

While in the bath, he wondered about the headache, how it had gone. Could be connected with the kitchen work being finished. The fake work, Judy's vandalism to give a reason for Jack being there. Such destruction. It had been painful. Well-made cupboards smashed. He had hated the sight of them. Was the headache partly psychological? No way of knowing, as he had bashed his head. And that could be it totally, or part of it.

The investigation, the remaining work for Judy now the kitchen work was over. Well, the real work. The prenup was the key. Say it enough times and it becomes an everyday word. Richard Ffrench had been secretly married to Lily. Why in secret?

A bath was good for thinking, lay back, add more hot water, ruminate. A means of control perhaps. She had her flat and shares so long as the marriage lasts. On top of that Richard Ffrench had made her the beneficiary in his draft will.

But the draft will hadn't been signed, so not legal. So Lily stayed a minor shareholder instead of the major. Did she even know any of this?

After the bath, Jack dressed in clean clothes. It was a summer's day, he would stroll along to the festival. Go to Mia's stall, see her while she was free. Bound to meet all sorts of people he knew in Forest Gate. Clients, friends. Then go to the house. He needed to talk to Judy.

Chapter 37

The festival was well underway when he arrived at Osborne Road, just a short walk from his flat. He was in T-shirt and jeans, and a baseball cap, with a backpack, containing a notebook, water and a few biscuits, just in case.

He'd try to find a book or something for Mia, to alleviate her jail time, from one of the stalls. Much as he didn't want to think about her sentence, it was unavoidable.

There it was, the festival ahead, filling the road. Last year it had rained, this year fine weather. Chancy, street festivals. Forest Gate festival had been held every year since 2000, except for two covid years. The street is cleared of traffic, all parked cars have to be out of the road by midnight the day before. Stall holders could drive in with their tables, gazebos and goods, but had to be away by 10 am, for an 11 o'clock kick-off.

There were barriers at the head of the street to stop traffic entering, but with a gap for pedestrians. Just pedestrians. 'We reclaim the street,' said Mia.

He was barely in the street, when a cheerful Asian woman in a hijab gave him a badge and timetable for the entertainment on the main stage and smaller stage. She seemed part of the information stall. Opposite two children were playing table tennis, next to them a drum band was practising.

The road ahead was packed with people and stalls on either side, most with gazebos. A man on stilts in Elvis costume was approaching. Jack knew him slightly, but couldn't think of his name.

He gave a thumbs up to Elvis, and called up to him: '*Don't be cruel to a heart that's true,*' clutching at his heart.

Elvis sang back, '*You ain't nothing but a hound dog, cryin' all the time!*'

Which Jack thought was unfair to one professing love, but you don't argue with a nine foot Elvis. He stretched up and they bumped fists. The long legged pop idol moved on.

Jack strolled, no hurry, and stopping where he fancied.

There was the stall for Forest Gate Community Garden. He'd been there a couple of times, they'd had some music events. The stall was selling plants, and had a cycle generator where a child was pedalling furiously and throwing off a mass of bubbles while being the energy to play *Puff the Magic Dragon*. Kids were painting discs with flowery patterns.

Next door was a stall with an old chap in a woolly hat, and a rack of books with a board advertising Forest Gate crime. Jack had enough local crime on his plate and gave it a miss.

Then an art stall, with people doing a collective painting stretched across three tables. A slim woman with black hair and striking red lipstick was touting for more painters. Jack kept back in case he should be enjoined to take up a brush.

And there was Tom coming down the centre of the road, colourful as ever, a yellow scarf and an orange cap. He had a green waistcoat and could have been one of the street performers.

'I thought you'd be at the wedding dinner,' said Jack.

'I'm taking a break,' he said. 'There's a guy at the Forest Gayte Pride stall I wanted to see, but he's not there. Might be later.'

'Can I ask you a question?'

'Ask away.'

'What did you think of the draft will?'

'Never saw it.' He flapped his hands to indicate his ignorance. 'Hardly the barest of ideas what was in it.'

'Maggie told me you had seen it.' She hadn't. This was a try on.

Tom threw up his hands. He was demonstrative, as if he had Italian roots.

'I shouldn't tell her anything,' he exclaimed. 'She's like the grapevine, say something to her and half the street gets it within the hour. OK, you got me, guv. I knew something was up as Dad's solicitor came a couple of times. So while Dad was having a bath, he always spends ages having a soak, I sneaked into his room, and saw it lying on the bed, full of crossings out. I took a photo of each page with my phone.'

'When was that?'

'Two days before Dad died. Or rather, was murdered by persons unknown, if we disallow Cliff. Or do you know by whom?'

'I have an idea who did it,' he said.

'Was it me?'

'You should know.'

'Not necessarily,' said Tom. 'Cliff doesn't know. He might've done, might not have done.'

A tea lady on stilts, pushing a trolley came by. Wearing a black dress with an apron, a cap like a doily, and holding a teapot; she was offering tea and cake to all and sundry, but not giving any.

'But I know it wasn't me did the deed,' said Tom. 'Tempted often enough. But never got round to it. I did tell Maggie that Dad was going to clobber us in his new will, but luckily for us, if not for him, it never got signed.' He leaned in closer. 'But that's very old news. Here's the stop press. Over dinner, the grapevine informed me that you are a private investigator.' He winked. 'Do you deny it?'

'No.'

Just as well it had come out, he thought. Now that the kitchen work was done, hardly mattered that he was outed.

'I thought you were too bright to be a builder, Jack.'

'That's a snobby thing to say,' he exclaimed, bristling. 'Why can't a builder be bright? Problems to solve, lots of skills needed. Harder than making up jingles.'

'And now I have offended you. Didn't mean to do that at all. But you are right, I shouldn't be such a snob. I am sure your job is a lot harder than making up slogans for chocolate bars which I get overpaid for. I apologise. Shake?'

He put out his hand. Jack shook it.

'No offence taken,' he said. 'And thank you for your help yesterday morning.'

'You were dead to the world, old pal. I thought you were drunk at first, slumped out like a corpse. Good to see you back on your feet. Don't forget to eat. Plenty of food stalls here. But going back to your dual role in our house. Might I say it stretches coincidence that a builder-cum-detective shows up just as the kitchen is vandalised.'

Jack realised Tom had sussed it.

'Was it you or Judy?' asked Tom.

'Not me,' said Jack.

'Thought as much. You are not the destructive sort. Not that I really know what sort you are, but you don't seem to be. But Judy, oh she can really get carried away. But I must love you and leave you, Jack, as I need to get back to the dinner for the speeches.'

He embraced Jack, and walked swiftly off.

Nice enough chap, thought Jack. Though he hadn't quite forgiven him for that crack about builders not being smart. As if the middle class brain is inherently superior.

Two female pirates on stilts came past, colourful in red headscarves and green waistcoats, false beards, their boat just big enough for the two of them, waving their cutlasses and shouting, 'Pieces of eight,' 'Ahoy landlubbers,' 'Out our way or walk the plank,' 'We're off to get treasure,' 'Fire a broadside.'

He chuckled at the litany, wondering at the same time how much they got paid. It must be awfully hard work walking up and down all day on stilts. They deserved whatever they got.

Jack was passing a second hand bookstall. Two tables of books. Might be something there for Mia. The stallholder was a friendly middle aged man, who Jack knew was usually at Forest Gate market, but had come here, obviously for the crowds. Jack had bought an astronomy book from him last year, and discovered that he was retired and all profits from his stall went to various charities. One answer to Mia's existential question.

'Have you got something about the environment?' he said.

Thoughtfully, the stallholder searched his books.

'How about this one?' He handed it over.

It was George Monbiot's *How did We Get Into This Mess?* Jack read the blurb. Looked heavy: politics, economics and climate change. Just right for Mia.

'It's for my daughter,' he said. 'How much?'

The stallholder waved away the price. 'It's free. I hear Mia is probably going to jail. A gift.'

Someone who knew him and his daughter, but how did he know she was going to jail? He didn't feel he could ask, though sometimes Forest Gate felt like a village. Jack tried to pay for the book, to contribute to his charities, but the stallholder wouldn't take it.

'Just say it's from me,' said the man. 'Someone has to save the planet.'

Jack didn't ask him his name as he felt he should know it. He thanked him and put the book in his backpack. Someone has to save the planet. Sure, but it wasn't him, but why wasn't it?

Apathy wrecks the planet, a slogan he'd seen on a T-shirt.

A little way up the road, the Dog Jammers were playing on the small stage. About ten of them, an assortment of guitars, an accordion, a bodhran drum. He knew some of them well, others vaguely. They were playing *Strawberry Fair*. An old English folk song. Jack knew the Bob Dylan version.

The Dog Jammers used to play at the Spotted Dog, hence their name. A very old pub, part of it dating back to Tudor days, now shamefully derelict. He liked their energy, their joy in playing. He'd seen them in the community garden a month ago. They segued into a Joni Mitchell number, *A Case of You*, a female vocalist taking over.

'Oh I love this song.'

It was Alison. She slipped her arm into his and they listened together. The singer had a good voice, and caught the emotion of the number.

Alison was quietly joining in, *'I could drink a case of you and still be on my feet.'*

She nudged him. Once that was true, but more than ten years ago. A lot of water under that bridge since. She was a teacher when they'd married but had gone up quite a few rungs since and now was headteacher of a primary school. Quite forceful was Alison, ambitious. She always had been.

The song ended.

'Let's go find Mia,' she said.

They wandered further up the street, arm in arm. They were passing the Woodcraft Folk stall. Mia had been a member and been introduced to eco politics there. Though he doubted any of her pals from those days were going to jail. A badge of honour or one of shame?

'Must eat something,' he said, indicating the Woodcraft Folk stall which was selling drinks and cakes as a fundraiser.

'I'll get it,' said Alison, and headed in to buy.

He didn't mind her paying; she earned twice what he made.

Alison was slim, her hair chestnut like Mia's, but much tidier, befitting of a head teacher. Both the same height. She wore jeans, a colourful T-shirt, sunglasses, and a fetching wide-brimmed straw hat. Always smart and ageing well.

Could that be said of him?

'Jack!'

She called him, needing his assistance. He went into the gazebo and took the proffered cake in a napkin and orange juice in a paper cup. Not quite kosher for a diabetic, but would keep the wolf away for a few hours. They wandered on, munching and drinking, saying hello here and there, as they went through the crowd.

How many were here, he wondered. Four thousand throughout the day, he'd heard of a past festival. But how could they know?

'How does having your daughter arrested affect you at school?' he said.

'Could be worse,' said Alison. 'Not exactly Bonnie and Clyde stakes,' said my deputy. Well, she hasn't shot up a bank, or even robbed an old lady. Getting more sympathy than brickbats. I shall keep my job.'

'Visiting her might be a pain,' he said.

'I hope the prison isn't too far away. There was a woman with two children at the school, had a husband in Parkhurst jail on the Isle of Wight. Used to take her a whole day to go there and back; the train fares were crippling. When the PTA heard, they paid them, but even so, she had to take the kids; it was inhumane to be so far away.'

Jack agreed, and hoped Mia wouldn't be in the back of beyond.

'There she is!' called Alison.

He saw her pitch, next to Newham Cyclists.

'Hi, Mum, Dad. You two back together?' she said with a wink as they approached.

'It's possible to stay friends,' said Alison primly.

'I've heard the two of you arguing,' she said.

'We are not arguing today,' said Alison. 'Are we, Jack?'

'Not yet. We watched Dog Jammers, and your mum treated me to an orange drink and cake at the Woodcraft Folk stall.'

'Drink up,' said Mia. 'We can use the cup and napkin. And oh yes, this is Sidra.'

'Hello,' said Sidra, an Asian girl in jeans and a green T-shirt they both wore saying, Save The Planet.

The stall had a table with various leaflets on it, and a bowl of badges. Over the table was a cardboard banner, well painted in various colours, saying Forest Gate Carbon Sinks.

'Sidra painted the banner.'

'It's good,' said Alison.

'Thank you,' said Sidra. 'It had to be recyclable. We didn't want anything professionally printed.'

Jack noted the leaflets on the table, but he wasn't going to argue that one.

In front of their table were three butler sinks, labelled *Reuse, Recycle, Junk.* Just the cupboard fittings were in reuse. Recycle was practically full. But Junk was spilling over with a full bin bag next to it.

Mia took their cups, and looked at them critically. 'Should be rinsed, but they are recyclable.'

'From Woodcraft Folk,' said Alison.

'They are improving,' said her daughter, and dropped them in the Recycled sink which was almost full. Mia pressed her boot on it. forcing the refuse down. She looked at their napkins. 'Quite clean,' she said. 'I am sure they can be recycled.' And dropped them in. 'You both get a badge.' She handed them one each.

Jack pinned his to his T-shirt, Alison to her hat.

'Thanks for breakfast,' said Jack.

'Thanks for coming to court,' said Mia. 'It's all right, Sidra knows I'm heading for the nick.'

'Got you a book,' he said and handed it over.

'Oh I like George Monbiot. Good choice. I'll take this to clink with me.'

Jack felt she was somewhat matter of fact, almost proud of the fact. As if it were a recommended college.

'We will come and visit,' said Sidra. 'We are proud of your daughter.'

'Thank you,' said Alison, though for once he felt she was stuck for words. She obviously didn't feel Sidra's pride. Jack himself was unsure. Maybe if she'd got away with it. He knew jail would not be at all pleasant. A shock rather.

'Where will you be tonight?' Alison asked Mia.

'Your place.'

'Good. I must get some shopping in. Talk to you tonight. Bye Jack, bye Sidra.'

And she left them. Jack stayed on, wanting to maximise his time with his daughter.

'Getting twenty-five quid for those fittings you gave me,' said Mia indicating the reuse sink. 'She's coming back to collect them at the end of the day.'

'Glad they can be useful,' he said.

Justifying his time getting them off the cupboards.

Two girls turned up with a box of refuse. Sidra took over.

'Let's sort this out,' said Sidra to the girls, 'what can be reused, what recycled and what is junk.'

She worked with the children going through their box, asking them about each items, before putting them into one of the sinks.

'How's your head?' said Mia to Jack.

'Headache's gone,' he said. 'And I slept like a baby.' Then he recalled. 'The guy at the bookstall wouldn't let me pay for the book. He says it's a gift.'

'I'll go and thank him later. Hey, Newham Cyclists are giving my bike an overhaul.' She indicated the busy station next to them, where several bikes were being worked on. 'Do you want my bike while I'm inside?'

'I haven't cycled for years.'

'You don't lose it, they say.'

'Yes, then. Let's get a bit greener.'

A boy came with a sack of plastic bottles, and then another with a cardboard box full. He'd get no more time with Mia. He kissed her on the cheek and left his daughter to get on with it. She'd be over his place in the week, she said, as she began working with the children. Sidra was emptying the junk into a bin sack. That sink was the stand out winner.

He left them. He had things to do at the house.

Chapter 38

Jack was heading for the house but waylaid by a local band on the main stage, the Foresters. They were playing the Beatles *Blackbird*. He'd had a short scene with one of the women singers. Didn't work out. He liked their music, but boy did they like volume. He had been in the Forest Tavern when they had been playing, and they had blasted the roof off.

But things to do. Somewhat reluctantly, he headed for the house. Going up the path, he saw Uncle Alec sitting on the front step, having a smoke.

'Couldn't you smoke in the garden?' he said.

Uncle Alec was in his brown suit, either the same he'd seen him in a few days ago, or one of several. He guessed the latter, Uncle Alec not being one for variety.

'Just kids smoking in the garden,' he said. 'And talking their nonsense.'

Not wanting a chat, Jack reckoned it best to cut to the chase.

'Did you get to see Richard Ffrench's draft will?'

Uncle Alec looked him sharply in the eye.

'You are a cop, aren't you?'

'I am a private investigator,' said Jack. The more times he said it, the more likely he was to believe it. And he might as well come clean, seeing that the kitchen work was done.

'What's a private eye doing here?'

With his cigarette hand he indicated the house behind him.

'I'm employed to find out who killed Richard Ffrench.'

'We all know who. Cliff confessed. That's history.'

'He's withdrawn his confession.'

Uncle Alec harrumphed. 'Doesn't work that way, young man. The cops have it. And once you have admitted it, you can't turn around and say I had a bad hair day. Didn't mean it, April Fool.'

The Foresters were playing *Don't Think Twice*. Jack tried again.

'Did you see the draft will?'

'Yeh, Dicky showed me it.' He brushed ash off his trousers. 'Nothing in it for me. But he wanted to screw the kids. Lack of respect, he said.' He laughed. 'Lack of respect did for him in the end. If it wasn't Cliff, who I'd still put my money on, it was one of the others strangled him.'

Jack wondered why they still allowed the old curmudgeon in the house. Habit, old times' sake? But then again, Jack reasoned, Uncle Alec managed the business and was a minor shareholder, so they needed to keep him sweet. Most likely.

Back to the draft will.

'What about Lily getting the lion's share?' he said.

'If she had have done, I'd have retired there and then. A jumped up housekeeper getting the works. What world is this?'

'Did you know Richard married her?'

'I did. Told me once when he was drunk. But he had her all tied up in a prenup. Enough questions, let me have a smoke in peace, copper.'

Jack didn't correct him, but went into the house. He could hear the hubbub, getting louder as he got nearer to the kitchen.

The kitchen was busy, looking like a kitchen should, smart cupboards, the new paint didn't show up on the old. Lily was dishing out pudding with four helpers. There were warming trolleys and piles of plates, the dishwasher running.

He went out to the patio, and took a seat. The marquee was full, the wall up facing him, almost like a cinema screen, rows of men in suits, carnations in their button holes and women in an assortment of colourful dresses. Smartly dressed children at their table. Catering staff, all women, were going between the tables, some collecting crockery, others handing out puddings.

Jack felt somewhat out of place amongst these besuited men and smart women in his casual wear. Like he hadn't been told it was a fancy dress do.

There was Judy, at the top table. She gave Jack a wave and came over.

She was wearing a low cut red dress, a yellow ribbon in her hair and high heels. They were in a different movie.

'How's your head, Jack?'

'Fine,' he said, feeling for the bandage. Still there.

'Do you want some food?' she said.

'Yes, please.' He had hoped there might be some going.

'I'll get you some.'

She went into the kitchen.

Something was going on in the marquee. Maggie, in a beautiful white dress, a lacy top and flouncy bottom, wearing some sort of coronet, had stood up, and picked up a guitar. Mo too, in a navy suit joined her with his guitar. There were cheers and clapping. A mic and stand was brought out, and the newly married couple stood in front of the top table and played.

No introduction, straight into it.

Mo played well but she was the star. And how could she fail, here, on her day. It was a love song, fitting for the day. One of hers he assumed as he didn't know it.

Judy came out of the kitchen with a tray of food. She ushered him to the patio table and placed the tray before him. Half a melon, a main dish and a fruit salad. Mia would almost approve, apart from the chicken in the main dish.

He ate, going straight for the main dish. Sprouts, baked potatoes, chicken and carrots. Just what the doctor ordered. Judy stayed with him, and they listened to Maggie and Mo.

The song finished, there was applause, he and Judy joining in, calls for more!

She held up a hand, silencing the wedding guests. 'That was a new song, written specially for my darling Mo. My husband!'

A cheer went up. Mo bowed and kissed Maggie. More cheering and clapping.

'We have one more song for you,' said Maggie. 'This one is for my brother Cliff, who you probably know is in Pentonville jail accused of murder. But he is innocent, I assure you. And we are working to get him out. Raise your glasses to Cliff.'

Glasses were raised. Maggie and Mo were passed a glass each.

'To Cliff.'

The audience echoed it back. Whether they believed it or not. It was just good manners at a wedding.

Maggie sang and played guitar, with Mo accompanying, the song dedicated to her brother. He joined in the choruses:

You were fitted up, you will not do the time, oh brother of mine, you will not do the time.

'Will he?' said Judy, turning to Jack. 'It's Saturday. Your deadline. Do you know who killed our father?'

He took a deep breath.

'I do. Give me half an hour and get Maggie, Mo, yourself, Tom, Uncle Alec and Lily to come into the sitting room.'

'What shall I say to them?'

'Say – the killer will be unmasked.'

'Wow!' She puffed out her cheeks. 'Before their very eyes. That is the big one, Jack. It will bring them all along, out of guilt or curiosity.' She kissed him on the cheek. 'I hope you have it right.'

He hoped so too.

Judy left to make the arrangements, while Jack finished his meal.

Chapter 39

They were all seated in the sitting room when Jack entered. A few minutes early, eager to know. Conversation stopped at his entrance. Maggie and Mo were seated on the sofa, Uncle Alec stretched out in an armchair, Lily, Tom and Judy on wooden chairs. He took one himself facing them all.

'Thank you all for coming,' he said.

'The fake copper is going to tell us who killed your dad,' said Uncle Alec.

'I am a private investigator,' said Jack. 'I had to be undercover.'

'You are a builder,' said Lily. 'You repaired the kitchen.'

Jack didn't want to get into that. Judy was looking uncomfortable.

'I am a private investigator,' he repeated. 'And a builder.'

The sitting room door opened, Nova stood in the doorway. In her suit, fitting in well with the wedding guests. He was the stand out casual.

'May I join you?' she said.

'Please do,' said Jack. He had phoned her twenty minutes ago. 'Some of you may already know Detective Sergeant Nova Taylor.'

'Why do we need another cop?' exclaimed Uncle Alec.

'Because one of us in this room killed Dad,' said Tom. 'And Jack is going to tell us who it is. Am I right?'

'Yes,' said Jack. Tom was helping out with his intro. So far, so good. 'Please take a seat, Nova.'

Should he be so familiar? Too late.

Nova took a chair between Judy and Tom, and took out her notebook.

Jack said to the room, 'Judy employed me to investigate the killing of Richard Ffrench.'

'We already know who did it,' said Uncle Alec.

'No we don't,' snapped Judy. 'Listen for once in your life.'

Uncle Alec harrumphed. 'I know what I know. It's cut and dried.'

'Shut up,' said Judy. 'And please listen.'

Jack could see Uncle Alec struggling to come up with a riposte, hissing, his fingers clawing at his thighs, but he held back, leaving the floor to Jack. He took a deep breath. There were holes in his argument, but he hoped he had enough logic.

'I started with an open mind,' he began. 'After the murder of Richard Ffrench, Cliff Ffrench was arrested. He confessed to the murder, but he has now withdrawn the confession. He says, it had been based on drug fuelled hallucination. So I demote him, from the killer to a suspect. As are all here, with the exception of myself and Nova.'

Jack waited for any objection but none came. He noted he had said Nova again instead of being more formal. Her cop role.

'You were all at Richard Ffrench's 70th birthday dinner,' he went on. 'Richard wasn't feeling well, so he left his guests and went to bed early. In the morning, he was found by Lily. There was no break in, so it had to be that one of you, guests at the dinner, murdered him.'

'I wasn't at the dinner,' said Lily. 'I cooked it.'

'But you were in the house,' he said. 'So I include you, along with Maggie, Mo, Judy, Tom, Cliff, and friend of the family Uncle Alec.'

'I am not your uncle,' said Uncle Alec.

'Don't be difficult,' said Maggie.

'How should I refer to you?' said Jack.

Uncle Alec smirked. 'It is Maggie's day, so I defer to her. I will be your uncle for the day.'

'Thank you,' said Jack. 'Uncle Alec, you had your reasons for wanting to kill Richard Ffrench. For the sharp practices that made you only a minor partner in the business, and for stealing your girlfriend.'

Uncle Alec waved a hand of dismissal. 'I would never have said all that to you if I knew what you were. A spy, a snoop. It's all ancient history, anyway, going back forty years.'

'Such things fester,' said Jack. 'And you couldn't evade him. He was effectively your boss as major shareholder in the business.'

'I don't hold grudges.'

'At his 70th birthday party, he held court, a successful businessman, in the family house with all his children present. How could you not hate him?'

Uncle Alec was silent. A silence that spoke volumes.

'We come to the draft will,' said Jack. 'In the existing will, the one that Tom, Judy, and Maggie have benefitted from, you each got over 20 per cent of the business. Cliff gets the same share, if he is found not guilty. But the draft will relegated you to 5%. With Lily as the major shareholder.'

No one spoke. Not even Lily, confirming what he had suspected, that she had seen the draft will too.

'The very existence of the draft will gives his children: Maggie, Judy, Tom and Cliff, a motive to kill your father. You all knew of the draft will. Supposed to be secret, but you all knew. Tom had seen it, photographed it, and told his brother and sisters about the content. Your father was going to humiliate his offspring, putting Lily in charge of the business, giving her this house too. I include you in this, Mo, as Maggie's loss would have been yours.'

'Don't belittle me, Jack,' said Mo. 'I have not married Maggie for money.' She put an arm round him. 'I love her.'

'Money trumps love,' Jack said.

'Oh how cynical, Jack,' said Maggie. 'I never would have thought that of you.'

'Cliff believed he killed his father,' Jack continued. 'And money was certainly a factor. He lived in his father's house, had to take his daily insults, and was making a poor living.

He certainly thought of doing him in, and, with all the drugs he was taking, believed he had actually done it.'

'But he didn't,' insisted Judy. 'With the help of the psychiatrist I appointed, he has come to realise it was all hallucinations, induced by drugs. He has withdrawn his confession.' She turned to Nova. 'Will that be considered?'

'Likely,' said Nova. She had been busy taking notes. 'It's all in the hands of the Crown Prosecution Service. They have been informed.'

'Each of Richard Ffrench's children is in the frame,' said Jack. 'You certainly weren't close to your father; you had assorted motives to resent him. You Maggie for being engaged to an Asian, you Tom for being gay, Cliff for being an unsuccessful artist, for being an artist at all, and you Judy for defending your twin brother and your sister. And of course the money, let's not forget the money. One of you, or perhaps it was a collective action, making it so unfair that Cliff took the rap for you all.'

'Why do you think so badly of us, Jack?' asked Maggie.

He ignored the barb.

'And you, Lily. You had your motives.'

'I did not,' she said. 'One of his ungrateful kids did it.'

'You were married to him.'

'Married?' exclaimed Tom. 'The first I have heard of it. Did anyone else know?' He looked to his siblings. 'Am I the only one in the dark here?'

'I don't believe it,' said Maggie. 'We all know you were sleeping with him, Lily. But he would never marry you.'

'Was he too good for me?' shot back Lily. 'Is that what you think? Me a housekeeper with broom and brush.' She smiled wryly. 'Unlike you, I kept him happy.'

'We don't need to know your bedroom tricks,' said Judy.

'You were married six years ago,' said Jack. 'Secretly. But there was a prenup.' Now so familiar with the term, it was as if it was the first word he had ever spoken. 'You were married certainly, but should there be a divorce, the prenup gives you nothing at all. You would lose your flat, your dividends, both granted to you just so long as you were married.'

'Or his widow,' said Lily. 'Which I am.'

'But the draft will,' Jack went on, 'would have given you this house on top of being in control of the business. And Richard Ffrench showed it to you. Did he not?'

'In bed,' sneered Maggie.

Lily did not reply.

'You would have been rich, seventy per cent of the business coming to you, along with this house. He went through the draft will with you, line by line. You as the victor. No longer the cleaner, the emptier of bins, no longer the lady who sweeps the stairs, but the winner of the sweepstake. But you made a mistake, Lily. You believed it had been signed. But in reality it was never going to be signed. Richard Ffrench left it around, on his bed while he was in the bath, so Tom would see it, and would tell his brother and sisters what Dad was up to with that scheming housekeeper.'

Jack turned to the siblings. 'It was just for show, written in all the proper legalese, but not signed and never would be. Just for show.'

'To get us to kowtow,' said Maggie. 'The old goat.'

'But he fooled you most of all, Lily. You thought it had been signed. He told you it had been. Led you on. That was Richard Ffrench all the way. Telling you what was coming your way, Lily. And so you believed that once he was dead, you would be the lady of the manor, owning the house and controlling the string of pharmacies. But what was to stop him changing it yet again? And so you killed him, Lily.'

He stopped, letting the accusation sink in. He had stuck in the knife. How would she react?

'Utter rubbish,' Lily exploded, standing up, as she declared to the room. 'A total cock and bull story. You can't prove any of it. It's all guesswork, from a builder, a stupid builder. I am not staying here a moment longer to be insulted. The murderer is one of these brats!' She swung round her arm, pointing out the family. 'One of these ungrateful low lives, living off their father's money, rooming here, rent free, and hating him. I am not staying in this horrible house a moment longer.'

She tore off her apron, threw it down, and was out the door. A few seconds later, the front door slammed

There was silence for fully half a minute. Thick with her anger and accusation, like a fog left in her wake.

'She is right about one thing,' said Jack. 'I know it, but I cannot prove it.'

'That's the way it goes,' said Nova. 'Speaking as a cop. I have been there, too many times. You know who did it but you haven't the proof. They know you know, but you can't damn well get them in the dock. It's hard, Jack. Boy do I know it, in too many cases, but you just have to live with it.'

Nova rose. 'Thank you for your company. It has been most illuminating. Well done, Jack. I must go back to the station and talk to my boss.'

She left them, the room remaining shell shocked.

Chapter 40

'Lily has sacked herself,' said Judy.

They had remained in the sitting room. Lily had stormed out, flinging out years of repressed insults. While Nova had left, more quietly, to talk to her superior. The others remained seated, shaking their heads at the revelations, attempting to take it in.

'Good riddance,' said Maggie. 'I never liked her. And being secretly married. She certainly fooled us all.'

'Quite a blast, she gave us,' said Tom. 'I never knew she had it in her.'

'To insult or to kill?' said Maggie.

'How long has she been holding in all that resentment?' said Judy.

'I doubt she'll ever be coming back,' said Mo. 'Now that we know. Excellent work, Jack.'

'She hasn't read the prenup properly,' said Uncle Alec. They turned to him, stretched out low in the armchair. 'The tail end says she must keep working as a housekeeper in this house until she is 65, or she forfeits her shares and her flat.'

'She has walked out,' said Judy. 'We didn't sack her. She's gone. Of her own accord. So she loses it all? Is that what you are saying?'

'Loses the lot. You can evict her from her flat,' said Uncle Alec. 'She had to remain the housekeeper until she was 65. But now she has fired herself. The ball is in your court. Personally, I would evict her.'

'Lily wouldn't dare come back,' said Mo. 'She has screwed herself.'

'And one more thing,' said Uncle Alec. 'A dividend is due in a month. My advice is this: don't give her a penny. Don't even notify her. Just stop her money.'

'A lawyer,' exclaimed Judy. 'My kingdom for a lawyer!'

'I need a drink, I need two drinks,' exclaimed Maggie rising from the sofa, still magnificent in her wedding dress, and pulling Mo to his feet. 'I can't take any more! Not on my wedding day. Thank you, Jack.' She kissed him on the cheek. 'But that is more than enough.'

'Brilliant,' said Mo. 'I am overawed. You smashed it, Jack, step by step, until she had nowhere to go. I am shocked and amazed.'

'Drink, Mo,' said Maggie. 'Come on. I am gasping. That was one hell of a ride, Jack.'

She and Mo left hand in hand.

'I need a smoke and a drink,' said Uncle Alec uncurling off the armchair. He stood. 'Cliff is off the hook, it seems. I dare say a couple of months in clink has done him no harm.'

Judy stared daggers at him, but said nothing, knowing the old man was too stubborn to be worth arguing with.

Uncle Alec took out his cigarettes and lighter, and left the room. He needed his double fix.

'Well done, Jack,' said Judy, once he had gone. 'You have more than earned your fee. A bonus is due. You didn't have long to investigate and I overdid the work you had to do. Forgive me. But you cracked it.'

'Though I can't prove it,' he said. 'I was just hoping she would break down when I accused her, incriminate herself. But she went the other way, declaring her innocence to the heavens.'

'She did, Jack, she more than did that,' said Tom. 'Pretty smart, all in all. For a builder.'

Jack didn't rise to the mockery, knowing this was how Tom worked. Hitting on your weak points.

'You leave my builder alone,' said Judy, pushing Tom away, and saying to Jack, 'Let's go out to the festival and listen to some music. But wait a minute. I need to sort the

195

kitchen out, now that Lily has gone AWOL. I have to make sure the hired help know exactly what they are doing. Or it will be total chaos in the kitchen, and we'll be up to our necks in leftovers and dirty dishes. Wait for me.' She set off, at the door turning, 'Do you two want a coffee?'

Both accepted her offer. And Judy left.

Jack blew out his cheeks, exhausted. Going round them one by one, pointing out why they were a suspect, and then homing in on Lily, had drained him of energy. Thank God it had worked out. Without proof, but believable.

He sank on to the sofa, stretching out his arms, head back in relief.

'Not so smart for a builder,' said Tom.

Tom had remained on a wooden chair, not having moved, cleaning his nails with a file.

'What wasn't?'

Was this just another insult, or was there more to it?

'Why did you leave me out?' said Tom.

'Leave you out of what?'

'Killing my father. What else?'

'You were a suspect. But if you had done it, you wouldn't leave Cliff stewing in jail. Would you?'

'He isn't going to stew in jail. Is he?'

'Not likely. Not now. But he might have done, if I hadn't accused Lily.'

'With no evidence.'

Jack thought rapidly at what Tom was implying. It could be so, it could be so. Or was it another one of his little jokes? It had to be. The adman playing games once more.

He asked the obvious question.

'Did you kill your father?'

Tom smiled. 'I did.'

Jack was taken aback. Another confession. It couldn't be so.

'That makes no sense. Why would you be telling me?'

He shrugged. 'There's only me and you here. If there were three, I would stay shtum. Silent as a statue. But I don't want you to be too clever, Mr Builder. It tends to make one arrogant.'

'How can I believe you?'

He shrugged. 'Believe me or not, it's all the same to me.' He smiled at Jack. 'Now to put you right. I hated my father. You know that much. His daily insults, his offers to pay for a gay cure. And the draft will, that topped it all. Giving us just crumbs while the lion's share went to that dreadful woman, and the house too. A horror story from a vindictive old man. My room is next to his. So easy to do it. A few minutes, that's all it took to strangle him. The best thing I have done in my life.'

Tom had lost his customary humour. He had just said that he had killed his father. Or would that be just another accusation without evidence? But his body language had not an ounce of playfulness about it.

Had Tom killed him or not? Jack was in utter confusion. Lack of evidence. In the uncertainty, could it be Tom? Had he cocked it up by accusing Lily? What had he done to her?

'Lily is going to lose her flat,' he said.

'Does she deserve it?' Tom said dismissively.

'Do you deserve this house?'

'Not at all. There are thousands of homeless people. I am one of the fortunate. And so has Lily been, until now. She has had her flat for years, rent free. It never was hers.'

Jack pondered that. It could have been hers, if she hadn't walked out. If he hadn't accused her. If he hadn't let the Ffrench siblings off the hook. He'd been in a rush. Wanted a result. Just like a copper.

'How long were you going to leave Cliff in jail?'

Tom shrugged. 'I hear two months in Pentonville has cleaned him up. Off drugs, he's got into prison art. A veritable rehab. And hey – you have most likely got him out.'

'You would have left him there to rot. Let him be sentenced to life imprisonment, if it came to it.'

'The fool confessed. I can't help that. He didn't need to at all. You have to pay for stupidity. I killed Dad because I hated him. Not to get a long stretch in jail.'

All wrong, all wrong. How could Jack have got into this cul-de-sac? Lily was the easy one, and he had gone for her, unwilling to pick one of the family.

What a mess!

Judy returned. She had a tray of coffees in paper cups and handed them out.

'Sorry I was so long,' she said. 'But it's hectic in the kitchen. I told them Lily had walked out. They said they can cope, she was too bossy anyway. I put one of the other women in charge and promised them all extra pay. So that's dealt with. You two are looking very serious. Have you finished your chat?'

'We have,' said Tom.

She took Jack by the arm.

'Let's go to the festival, Jack. Chill out and listen to some music. Bring your coffee.'

Chapter 41

The wedding was going on for another few hours when Jack left. The festival on the street had packed up, there were just a few people around collecting litter. Jack was invited to stay at the wedding where there was dancing to a small combo, but he was mentally exhausted, and wouldn't fit in with his casual wear at a wedding.

Or in his mood. He was devastated.

Not the mood to be at an occasion awash with booze. Max had warned them often enough. Avoid such occasions, especially if down in the dumps. Jack knew for certain that if he stayed, he would get drunk. Utterly blotto. Which would solve nothing. Pass some time, get him out of the hell he was in, for him to wake up in one worse. He had failed, made worse with the praise heaped upon him.

Jack went home.

He had a shower, no help. Couldn't be bothered to cook, had a big bowl of Mia's muesli. Tried watching TV, but couldn't concentrate, one channel after another. His brain had turned to mush.

He phoned Nova.

'Hello, Jack.'

'I am having doubts about Lily,' he said.

'We are not going to charge her.'

'I think it might be Tom.'

'Stop it, Jack. You'll end up accusing the whole household. First it's Cliff, and then it's not Cliff, then it's Lily, and now it's not Lily, it's Tom. You can't just throw names out like that. No one is going to believe anything you say.'

He got that. He could blow his reputation with this too hasty pinpointing. For the time being, nobody knew he'd cocked up, bar Tom. And Tom wouldn't be speaking out or writing a confession.

Jack had been paid to clear Cliff, how was that faring? One win, he hoped.

'What's happening to Cliff?' he said.

'We've told the Crown Prosecution Service about our doubts. And they are considering the matter. That's all I can tell you. They might drop the charges. The case against Cliff rested mostly on his confession. He's withdrawn it, as you know. And now with the Lily confusion, it must be sowing more doubt on his guilt. But please don't say anything more about Tom. You proved it was Lily. OK, thin on evidence, I agree, but I have told Fayyad it was Lily. Don't hit me with Tom. Or I'll go crazy.'

This was pointless. He'd been too hasty with Lily, and now Nova wasn't listening. The cops dilemma, keep the accused in clink, deny new evidence, or you'd have to admit a mistake.

His own dilemma. Ace cock-up.

Jack thanked her for her help and rang off. He still had a couple of sleeping tablets given to him by the hospital. He took them.

And slept the night away.

In the morning, he was feeling a little better. Lily would not be charged, but likely he had lost her her flat and her share in the business. She shouldn't have insulted the family and she shouldn't have walked out. All very well to say, but it was him, he had accused her of murder. That might set anyone yelling a torrent of insults at anyone nearby.

Cliff's case, though, was looking better. One good thing. It was like a see-saw, what Lily had lost Cliff was gaining. Jack had muddied the water by making the case against Lily. But without a shred of hard evidence. All supposition.

The bell rang. He went down. It was Judy in her running gear, shorts, trainers, and T-shirt.

He invited her up, started making tea, but they went to bed instead. Anything but talk.

200

Chapter 42

Three Weeks Later

Jack and Judy travelled up by train. They couldn't talk much on the journey with the rattle over the tracks and the busy carriages. As if both had agreed, it was not a good idea to talk of prison and murder on a train journey. He hadn't seen much of her in the last week. She had been organising an event in Suffolk, but now had a couple of days off.

They alighted and had a ten-minute walk on a quiet road.

'What is happening about Lily and the flat?' he said.

'Well you may ask. All sorts of complications,' she said. 'She is taking us to the tribunal for constructive dismissal. Our lawyer says she has a good case. We can't claim she's a murderer, as there's no evidence, just the possibility that she killed Dad. The police aren't arresting her which weakens it, anyway. Not that we want to go to the tribunal. She was married to Dad, so making matters ultra complicated. We are thinking it's best to concede, reluctant as we are, and give her the flat.'

'And her shares?'

'Also complicated. Lily has hired a lawyer and is threatening to sue us. Our lawyer says it would be a lot cheaper and better for our reputations to just give in, as she could well win, what with us accusing her of murder with little evidence. So it looks like Lily gets away with it.'

Jack was relieved that Lily was fighting. And winning. He had been responsible for the family efforts to strip her of the flat and her shares. She was innocent. But someone else was getting away with murder.

'Suppose, for argument's sake say, Tom killed your father.'

'What do you mean?'

'Bear with me and suppose. How would you deal with it?'

She thought for a few seconds. 'I'd probably say good luck to him, considering his relationship with Dad. Is that too honest?'

'Probably.'

'He is family.'

And Lily isn't. She was secretly married to their father, and the draft will had scared the family soppy. Lily would have ruled the roost if it had ever been enacted.

He'd done a poor job, but he might get away with it. If Lily, as likely, keeps the flat and her shares, if he had muddied the water enough, so Cliff gets the charges dropped. Looking likely too.

What were his excuses for his wrong-headed investigation? It had been a rushed job. Too much building work, working late, Mia in court, getting over being dumped by Nova; all in all, too little time for a proper investigation. There was a major lesson here. With lack of evidence, have the guts to admit you don't know.

'Any news on Cliff?' he said.

'He's still surprisingly cheerful, considering where he is. Our lawyer says he might be released in the next week or two. But believe this. Cliff wants to stay at least another month to complete his art project. Remember, his prison drawings to make a book. The governor is happy with the book idea. It's almost a joke. Imagine wanting to stay in clink.' She laughed. 'I can't get over it.'

Cliff happy at least. Jack considered what might have happened, if with all suspects together in the sitting room, he had accused Tom of the murder and not Lily. She was the easy victim. Tom wouldn't be easy at all. His two sisters would have charged in like the cavalry to their brother's defence, crushing Jack under their hooves.

Evidence, evidence. No accusations without evidence.

She pointed ahead. 'Is that the prison? Quite smart, nothing like as gruesome as Pentonville.'

This was Bronzefield women's prison. Not too far away, all considered, just outside of London. Alison had already visited and said the journey was easy enough by train from Forest Gate. Go to Waterloo, she'd said, then change at Staines. Less than two hours including the walk to the prison.

They went to the visitors' centre, where the officer there checked that they were down for a visit. Mia was allowed four a month. They showed IDs, signed forms, and wore a wristband, all reminiscent of Pentonville. Jack left two eco books for Mia at the counter, as well as a novel Alison had selected. They had to be checked for contraband. Could be many days before they eventually got to Mia.

Again there were lockers, for phones, handbags, Jack's wallet, though both kept credit cards as snacks could be bought.

They were taken with other visitors to the visitors' hall where Mia was waiting at a table, Judy having bought a tray with three coffees and some cakes. The hall was more colourful than Pentonville and there were more children running around. Jack was surprised to see men warders as well as women.

Jack hugged Mia, Judy too.

'So how's it going?' he said.

'This place is an education,' she said. 'So many pregnant women. I haven't been beaten up yet but there are some real tough women here. Stay low key, be helpful. Won't always work as there are a lot of mental health cases. I am surprised how many women can't read or write. One woman comes to me to write letters for her. Real personal stuff, almost embarrassing.'

'Your hair has been cut,' he said. 'It's good. Shorter.' He didn't say tidier, but thought it.

'They do a hairdressing course here for inmates. Thought I'd take advantage.'

203

'What are the screws like?' said Jack.

Mia shrugged. 'Some good, some bad. I've only been in for ten days, but boy you learn quick. I listen to those who have been here a while. Who know the ropes. Food is horrible, but you can buy stuff. Mum keeps my card topped up.'

'What about your cell?' said Judy.

'Basic, concrete floor, concrete walls. Two of us. I am lucky that Mandy is my cellmate. She was on the protest with me. If she wasn't, I'd rather be on my own. There's a toilet, a sink, bunk beds, a TV. I have never watched so much rubbish, but if one watches the other has to. The cell is too small to ignore it. Every so often, one of the women kicks off, and we are all locked in. Or jobs get cancelled because of lack of staff and it's stay in your cells.' She laughed. 'Ten days and I am sounding like an old lag. My turn now. Tell me about you two. Has he taken you out on the Flats with his telescope?'

'Yes, but it's a good job it isn't far. Cloudy most of the time we went. A view of the moon, and managed to catch three of the four main moons of Jupiter.'

'Well, well,' said Mia. 'You might last. It's always Dad's big test. Out on the Flats. Dad worked at your house, didn't he?'

'And solved a crime.'

No I didn't, thought Jack. Cocked it up completely, though he would never tell Judy that.

'Your mum phoned the governor, I hear,' said Jack to get off the subject.

'Oh, she sure did. Got through too, had quite a chat about the education here. Embarrassing though, Mum being a Head and pulling strings. My study in the library counts as work. But it's tricky working with no internet. Mum got me an e-reader, special privilege. She has to load new books on it, I can't.' She shrugged. 'It's prison. Life is bearable, so far. It's the rules that get you down. You have to have movement slips for everything. You queue to get them printed out, queue for food, queue for exercise. There's a bike repair workshop. They repair them for charities. I want to get on that, but it's full. I'm on the waiting list. My big bugbear is the noise in this place. All that concrete, bang bang bang outside your cell. Blaring music, TVs, women screaming for their medication. Mum bought me earplugs a week ago but they are still at reception. Each one being examined for drugs, I bet.'

They chatted on, about life here, what Mia was reading, about what was going on in Forest Gate. Mia was curious about Judy's job as an event organiser, what bands she signed up. Judy promised to get her and a friend in to one of the festivals once she was out.

If we are still together, thought Jack.

The hour was up. Next week, two of Mia's eco pals were coming to visit. The week after, her mum, then Jack again. Four visits a month soon filled up.

They hugged Mia. And split asunder, Mia back inside, Jack and Judy to the free world.

It was a relief to be out in the open air, without all the keys, the rules, and the forms. Difficult to know what it was really like inside without experiencing it. Likely, very different if you were black, lesbian, disabled. So many screws and all their prejudices. It amused him that Alison had phoned the governor, just like Alison. Head teacher's privilege.

'It costs over 60 thousand pounds a year to keep each prisoner in there,' said Judy. 'I looked it up.'

'All those screws have to be paid,' he said. 'The office staff, tutors, food, laundry. And it's a private prison. Profit has to be made.'

'She's coping.'

Jack nodded. Six months was Mia's sentence. With good behaviour she'd be out in three. Watch lots of TV, read her books, and do what she was told. And hope no one beats her up.

They went to a supermarket and bought food for a picnic, having prepared for this beforehand, bringing cups, spoons and knives from home. The latter both wooden or they'd never have got into the prison.

Judy, using her phone app, got them to the bank of the Thames. They'd have a walk by the shore, and a picnic. A sunny day with lots of flowers in the hedgerow. Jack didn't know what they were, just flowers and colour, but Judy pointed out cow parsley, purple loosestrife and rosebay willowherb. He was impressed. His limit was dandelions and daisies.

They strolled along hand in hand. The river was half the width out here than it was in London, the sun shining off the wavelets on the water, raised by passing rowers and motor boats. More stately, a narrowboat came by, hardly faster than they were walking. They settled on a patch of grassland by the side of the river, and laid out their picnic.

They had barely begun when she said:

'Who really killed him?'

An unexpected question. Demanding a careful answer.

In the end he said, 'Not Lily. I made a major mistake there. A rush job. I am glad she is fighting back. She should get her flat and the shares. I'd like to apologise to her, but I am sure she'd slam the door in my face.'

'I gave you too much building work.'

'And an impossible case. Two months had gone by, with Cliff in jail. I had my daughter in court to deal with, I bashed my head, those damned cupboards, and Maggie sending threatening emails to herself.'

He didn't add a busted love affair with Nova, but it was certainly a factor. A big distraction when it came to clear thinking.

'Why did you employ me?' he said.

'To clear Cliff.'

'And did I?'

She shrugged. 'You muddied the water. Added uncertainty. He'll be out in a few weeks.'

'Your psychiatrist did more for Cliff than I did. Showing him it could have been a drug-fuelled hallucination.'

'Cliff is fighting his case. Pleading not guilty, retracting his confession and, yes, claiming it was a hallucination.'

'But he is not sure. He thinks he might have strangled his father.'

'That's because he did.'

Jack was unsure what he had heard her say.

'Are you saying he actually did it?'

'I am.'

He was gasping. All that misplaced effort, he'd been hired to clear a guilty man. If this was so. It was a maze and he was lost.

'How do you know?'

The picnic forgotten. Neither were eating. The river and the boats might not have been there, the clouds and sky rubbed away as if on glass. This could have been in the dullest of dull rooms. It was the words, her face and her body. The truth or falsity of them.

'Because I saw him. I had come upstairs to get him,' she went on. 'He'd left the dining room. All evening he had been shifty and restless, giving one-word answers, if speaking at all. I knew he went up to get stoned, and I was tempted to leave him to it. There was just me and Tom at the table. Mo and Maggie had driven back to Mo's flat, Uncle Alec had taken a cab, Lily left too. But I had a sense, call it twins tele-pathy, that Cliff was not just getting stoned.

'The master bedroom door was open. I went in, and saw Dad laid out on the bed and Cliff leaning over him. I knew what Cliff was up to. I came in closer, and I saw him tugging at the wire round Dad's neck. Dad was gurgling, fingers round the wire, trying to pull it away, his body jerking. And then he stopped struggling with a final gasp. Cliff stepped back, staggered a couple of steps and collapsed in a heap.'

Jack was silent for half a minute, taking it in. Tom had confessed to him. What was Judy up to? Telling him it was now Cliff, after everything.

'You saw it all,' he said at last.

He could barely believe what he was hearing, but could detect no hint of a lie in her body language.

'I was concerned for Cliff. Having done what he'd come up for, the strength rushed out of him like a burst tyre. He was collapsed on the floor. I took off his tie and undid his shirt. He was out to the world. I went to look at Dad, and I saw he was recovering. A pained breathing coming through, his eyes were open, he was clutching at his neck.' She turned to Jack. 'I couldn't leave him like that. Knowing. Could I?'

Jack knew what she was about to say. The horror of that bedroom. Twins together.

'So I finished him off.'

They were silent. The river returned, a rowing eight came past, the cox calling out, one two three, one two three. Eight bodies in rhythm. Tuned muscle and exertion as the oars swung in time, oblivious to a confession of murder.

'Tom came in,' she went on. 'Saw it all at once. I had the wire in my hand. Cliff was snoring on the floor. And Dad was dead. We didn't need to speak. It was obvious what had been done. We carried Cliff into his bedroom. He would sleep till Kingdom Come. Tom ushered me away, telling me to go home and throw the wire somewhere far off. I left him cleaning up the bedroom, wiping prints off the door handle, and I drove home. I can't remember what I did with the wire. Perhaps hypnosis would tell me.'

She stopped, having said it all. They didn't speak for a while. He staring at the woman he did not know, she half smiling, waiting for him.

'You seem almost proud of it,' he said.

'I did what I had to.'

'Why did you tell me?'

She shrugged. 'I was tired of your guilt. As if you had done it. No, it was me all along, Jack. Don't worry, Lily will be all right.'

'And Cliff will get off.'

'He didn't do it.'

Jack was angry, he was bewildered. How could he and Judy recover from her revelation? How could he sleep with her after what she'd said to him. Or even face walking back to the station with her, and then the journey to Forest Gate sitting side by side.

He recalled her frenzy, rushing about the kitchen smashing the cupboards with glee. She could easily be roused to destruction. Was her confession a way of testing his mettle? If so, he had failed her. And she had failed him.

Not that he had expected their affair to be long lasting. She had money to burn and liked dressing up for occasions, while casual was his any occasion wear. Such things might be worked round, but she had murdered her father. And set him up for a fall.

'I thought you would be with me, Jack. Like you were with the smashed cupboards.'

'That's furniture. I'll lie for cupboards anytime.'

'Especially when I am paying you over the odds. How much do you want for a hit?'

That was a low blow, making it clear who had the money.

'I was going to give you cash to expand your business,' she went on, a hint that she still might.

'Pay me as much as you like and I will still know you killed your father.' Then quickly, he had to say it quickly. 'Keep your money. It's tainted.'

'My father was wicked.'

'And what are you?'

They were staring at each other across the forgotten picnic. Two stately swans floated by unseen.

'You tell me.'

'There's ice in you, Judy. Hatred for anyone that crosses you.'

She smiled wryly. 'I am a realist, Jack. I am a winner.'

What had she won, he reflected. Money, a house. But she would not win him. He thought of Mia, in jail for her principles. Judy would not buy him, or how could he face his daughter?

Judy stood up, looking at him as if she might say something important, some words of mitigation. But there was nothing to be said. Neither could stretch out a hand to the other. She had said too much.

She hitched up her backpack and faced him.

'Jack.' He looked up at her. 'You have just turned down fifty thousand pounds.'

He laughed in disbelief.

'Why not say one million, if I am not going to get it?'

As he grinned, at the money, at her gall, she turned away and strode up the river path. She should have given him the money first, he thought, then confessed. That would have really tested him.

Just as well she didn't.

He watched her, a slim figure walking swiftly, growing smaller. Was she regretting her confession or pleased to get it out? A means to be rid of him and save all that money, if it was real money. Jack took up a yogurt from the forgotten picnic, tore off the lid, and absently, without tasting it at all, spooned it up, watching her progression, as if it were a movie, breathing steadily as if he'd just done twenty push-ups, until Judy was tiny, avoiding a cyclist, and disappearing round a bend in the river.

Out of his life.

He ate some crisps, some nuts, feeling numb. A couple arm in arm passed by, laughing. They said hello to him, and he offered them the remaining yogurts. He would never have got them home in this warm weather, he said. They asked him if he was sure, he assured them he was, not straying into a tale of murder, bribery and a broken affair. The couple took them with the spoons, and with a parting wave, walked on.

Jack stayed for some time sitting on the bank, watching the boats and the birds. Mia was OK. That was most important. He would have to be. He had messed up, but so had the cops. There was no point telling Nova what he'd heard today. He had given her too many versions for this one to take root.

The wrong people had got rich, and he had accepted dirty money. All he could say was that he didn't know. There were lessons to be learnt. The importance of evidence. Was Judy telling the truth or spinning another yarn? Either she or Tom were lying. They can't both have killed their father. Tom, though, wanted to put Jack down, and Judy's story had detail. It said why Cliff thought he could have strangled his father. He had all but done so, in her version. Either way, she, Tom and Cliff were involved in the murder.

He would believe her. For the little it counted what he believed.

Justice was fickle. Some got her blessing, some yearned for it, others evaded her completely. There would always be those who got away with murder, no matter how perfect we want the world to be, with the guilty always punished and the innocent going free.

What never world might that be?

A buzzing in his pocket shook him out of his reverie. Jack took out his phone. A text from Alison:

I hope your and Judy's visit to Mia at Bronzefield went well. Can you ask Judy to contact me? We need a marquee for the school fete.

Jack chuckled.

An hour ago, he would have asked Judy. Not now. Or ever. He thought of texting: *we have broken up*. But it was too soon, too raw.

Bottle of whisky? No, no, no. Get used to being alone, mate. Sometimes that was the best way to be. Jack didn't need Max's wisdom to see that path. Better than being shackled to someone you hated. No self pity, he was alive, his daughter was coping, and the rights and wrongs of the case were out of his hands. He had money in the bank, no matter where it had come from. And there was work tomorrow, repairing a brick wall.

Like his mother might say, count your blessings. A hack-neyed phrase but he wasn't in clink and he had work.

On his phone, Jack found his location on a map, to get him to the nearest station. He set off, walking slowly down the river, the opposite way from her, looking at the birds, the flowers, even if he didn't know one from another, the flow of the water, the passing boats, and up at the infinite sky where the stars were waiting. There all along, but blotted out by sunlight. No bottle of whisky was needed to make life bearable. He had learnt that much. Put one foot in front of the other. And make the best of what comes your way.

Thank you!

I am grateful to every reader who finishes one of my novels. I have taken you on a journey which I hope you have enjoyed. There are plenty of things you could have been doing, other than reading this book. So, thank you for your time. If you liked *Jack and the Vandals*, here's what you can do next:

I'd appreciate a review. In that way, you can help me tell other readers about my books. Without reviews authors get few sales. So I'd be grateful for your review to help this series get on the move.

You can get a FREE ebook of *Murder at Any Price* if you sign up for my readers' list. You may give it to a friend if you wish. When you sign up for my readers' list you will receive my regular newsletter. This will give you news about me, what I'm reading, and tell you about my future books, PLUS a variety of giveaways.

Sign up at my website:
DerekSmithWriter.com

Books by DH Smith

Jack Bell

These are all standalone novels and can be read in any order. They are:

- *Jack of All Trades*
- *Jack of Spades*
- *Jack o'Lantern*
- *Jack By The Hedge*
- *Jack In The Box*
- *Jack On The Tower*
- *Jack Recalled*
- *Jack At Death's Door*
- *Jack At The Gate*
- *Jack In The Dust*
- *Jack At The Lodge*
- *Jack In The Garden*
- *Jack Fell Down*
- *Jack In Clink*
- *Jack Takes A Walk*
- *Jack And The Vandals*

Other Books
Writing A Crime Novel

Books by Derek Smith

All my books, other than the *Jack of All Trades* series and *Murder at Any Price*, are written under the name Derek Smith.

Fantasy
Hell's Chimney
The Prince's Shadow

Other Books
Strikers of Hanbury Street (short stories)
Catching Up (poetry)

Young Adult Novels
Hard Cash
Half a Bike
Fast Food
Frances Fairweather Demon Striker!

Children's Novels
The Good Wolf
Feather Brains
Baker's Boy

For Younger Children
The Magical World of Lucy-Anne
Lucy-Anne's Changing Ways
Jack's Bus

About the Author

I live in Forest Gate in the East End of London. In my working life, I have been a plastics chemist, a gardener and a stage manager before becoming a professional writer. I began with plays, working with several theatre companies, and had a few plays on radio and TV, as well as on the stage.

In the early 80s I became involved in running a co-operative bookshop and vegetarian café in Stratford, where I learned to cook, and had my first go at writing a novel. The first was a mess, and, after too many rewrites, binned. The transition from drama to novels took me a couple of years to get to grips with.

My first success was a young adult novel, *Hard Cash*, published by Faber. Buoyed up by this, I stuck with children's work, did school visits, and made a hand to mouth living as a full time author, topped up with some evening class work in creative writing at City University and the Mary Ward Centre in Holborn. A few adult fiction titles appeared from time to time, between the children's list, and I have since been working more in that direction with my *Jack of All Trades* series.

DerekSmithWriter.com

This book was designed
by Lia at NewRadical

www.ingramcontent.com/pod-product-compliance
Lightning Source LLC
Chambersburg PA
CBHW071132200626
46817CB00018B/2783